MORTAL RUIN

John Malcolm was born in Manchester and read
Engineering at Cambridge when not rowing for
Lady Margaret Boat Club. He has worked as a
salesman for textile machinery and as an international marketing consultant, and travels
extensively worldwide.

He and his wife, a picture restorer, have
always been interested in antiques and used to
supplement their income by selling antique
furniture bought at daybreak on Sunday mornings in London's East End. This led to their
becoming founder members of the Antique
Collectors Club and to authorship of several
price guides to Victorian and Edwardian
furniture.

D1144325

By the same author

GOTHIC PURSUIT
WHISTLER IN THE DARK
THE GWEN JOHN SCULPTURE
THE GODWIN SIDEBOARD
A BACK ROOM IN SOMERS TOWN

JOHN MALCOLM

Mortal Ruin

FONTANA/Collins

First published in Great Britain by
William Collins Sons & Co. Ltd 1988
First published in Fontana Paperbacks 1989

Copyright © John Malcolm 1988

Printed and bound in Great Britain by
William Collins Sons & Co. Ltd, Glasgow

Chapter One

The immigration officer at O'Hare was very affable. He took my passport, after I had politely waited in line, and grinned at me as he thumbed the document open. His eyes took in my face, my dark suit, white shirt and sober tie. They flicked back to my broken nose before he saw the briefcase in my hand.

'You're here on business,' he said factually, checking my visa and my immigration forms before picking up one of those curious, metal, spring-loaded stamps they use, the sort that have only survived in Government departments and airports the world over.

'That's right.'

'What kind of business?' He moistened the stamp casually, on a pad.

'I'm a banker. An investment banker.'

To my left, the thick lines of arriving passengers rustled in half-impatient expectation. Chicago is a busy airport, the busiest in the world. Everyone seems to be in a hurry. I looked at the immigration man in his white short-sleeved shirt, noting the American vest beneath, with its rounded neck, an undershirt of a type you never see anywhere else, and wondered how long he would be.

'You investing in Chicago, Mr Simpson?'

I smiled at him. 'Possibly. We already have to some extent. We work together with Owens, McLeod and Casey.'

His eyebrows raised themselves a little and his head bobbed in a nod. Others may not have heard of

Owens, McLeod and Casey, but locally they are a well-known firm of investment bankers, established in the nineteenth century, part of Chicago's business tradition. His face registered approval. 'Uh-huh.' The stamp banged down and my passport, with its papers, came back over the counter. 'Well, in that case, if you're here on business, you won't want to hang around. Welcome to Chicago, Mr Simpson. Hope you have a successful stay here.'

That's what I like about America. In half the airports of the world, if you make the mistake of saying that you're there on business they peer at you suspiciously, eyes narrowed. What business? they demand to know. Why? Who with? How much are you going to make? Have you got a business visa? What tax will you pay, which one, that is, of several they've got; you can't leave until we tax you; and so on. Not in America. In America business is business, refreshing thought, and you can get on with it. They really do believe that what is good for business is good for America and there you go; don't muck about, get on with it, you should be busy if you're here on business.

It was the same in the Customs hall. My suitcase came up on the conveyor. I took it and my briefcase to a Customs official, planked them down in front of him and handed over the declaration form. He looked at me. He was large, his grey shirt straining into the waistband of his dark trousers. He looked as though he lived on beef and ice-cream, happy days, none of your modern dietary fads. Our eyes met in friendly fashion.

'Here on business?' He held the declaration form at arm's length in order to read it better.

'I am.'

'In that case – ' he leant forward and scribed squiggles with a piece of yellow chalk – 'you won't want to hang around here, will you? Carry on through, right over there. Door on the right. Have a nice stay in Chicago.'

'Thank you.'

'You're welcome.'

So there I was. Just like that. I strode through the exit door and out into the arrival hall milling with people. I was feeling extremely cheerful. It had been a good flight, on time, quite comfortable. I hadn't drunk much. I was a bit stiff, one knee particularly, and slightly dazed, as one always is after eight hours or so on a plane, but I like America and I'm usually exhilarated by going there. Since Andy Casey had promised to meet me at the airport, I was entirely relaxed about getting to my hotel and down to business after a wash and brush-up. Everything was going to plan. I scanned the crowd, looking for his lean figure, his freckled face among the mob.

He wasn't there.

An impatient traveller half-collided with me from behind and I moved forward, apologizing. Something must have delayed Andy, or perhaps he'd sent a driver if an urgent bit of business had come up. I pushed gently through the people between me and the glass doors at the exit which gives to the roadway outside, where taxis and limos and private cars jostle with buses and courtesy vans. A dark-suited chauffeur with a peaked cap stood near the taxi desk inside the doors. I moved across to him and put my suitcase down for a moment as I spoke to him, holding on to my briefcase.

'Excuse me – are you from Owens, McLeod and Casey?'

He shook his head. 'Nope. Not me.'

I held up a placatory hand. 'Sorry.'

A man bustled in through the swing doors and I turned quickly in case it should be Andy because the shape was like him, over six feet, fairly lean and active, but it wasn't. I wondered if we had given the wrong flight details to each other somehow and turned back to pick up my case, a standard large green Antler fibreglass job with a band I put round it for identification because so many modern suitcases look alike.

It wasn't there.

My stomach went hollow. The suitcase wasn't there. I blinked at the empty spot, now crossed by striding people in a kaleidoscope of clothes, hurrying by. My case, I thought, slowly at first, then with rapidly-cranking speed as the adrenalin began to flow, my case, this is happening to me, not to someone else, my case has gone, just like that, everything had been going so well, I put it down there and someone has picked it up –

Luckily, I caught sight of it out of the corner of my eye. There was a grey-suited man carrying it, quite conventionally in his right hand, arm straight down, walking normally, not too fast, not too briskly, away among the crowd, no, he was turning now, going towards the exit doors further down to my right.

'Hey!' I called out, not too loudly, not wanting to make a fuss, you know how we English are, don't want to draw attention to ourselves or make a scene, but a case is a case when you're abroad and this one had all my gear in it. 'You've got the wrong case! That's – '

He went straight through the doors and outside without altering the rhythm of his walk at all, deaf to the world. I plunged out of the nearest door on to a pavement dotted with people carrying their own luggage, moving towards bus stops, cab ranks, God knew what. Fresh air pricked my nose.

'Hey! My case!'

He was slender, of medium height, not remarkable in any way, not striking, in fact very unremarkable, almost camouflaged by his conventionality. He went away from me at what seemed to be an increasing pace, weaving skilfully through the people and the pillars of the building, the signposts and odd kiosks, crossing towards a multi-storey car park opposite, beyond some roadworks that scattered earth and barriers between the park and the airport terminal.

'Oy!' I roared after him, as he nipped between barriers towards a pair of doors.

No one paid the slightest attention. I gripped my briefcase tightly in my right hand and sprinted after him, cursing at a twinge from my stiff knee, skidding past people and half-apologizing as I brushed them. I had a mental image of myself galloping up to this mistaken bag-carrier as he put the Antler into the boot of his car, parked inside the multi-storey somewhere; I didn't want to be too aggressive but if I didn't move fast I was going to lose my clothes and some papers, not important papers because those were all in my briefcase, but useful papers none the less. A sense of unreality, of unpreparedness, persisted in me.

The roadworks had striped barriers round them. Beyond the clutter of equipment and planking, the car park's concrete walls had various openings and doors in them. I pelted after the grey man down a short length of asphalt that led to a pair of swing doors made of rubber or plastic, the sort that fork-lift trucks can butt through en route to pallet racks or similar destinations. Without thinking, I hurled myself through them, only to stop short.

There were three men just beyond the doors. Behind them stretched a cavernous area of empty garage, devoid of cars. The grey-suited man was bending over my suitcase. Beside him stood a big fellow in a lumber-jacket and jeans. To his left was another man, nearer to me, a slender black man with a grizzled non-shave to his face and a greasy peaked cap on his head. He grinned as I drew up, panting, in front of them.

'I'm afraid you've made a mistake,' I gasped at the grey-suited man. 'That's my case. You picked it up in the hall. By mistake.'

He straightened up and the three of them faced me. None of them spoke. Suddenly, I felt uneasy. Behind me were the big rubber doors, cutting off the outside world. In front of me was this oddly-assorted threesome, the cavernous garage area, a gritty concrete floor. I cleared my throat, getting my breath back.

'That's my case,' I said again, less firmly, but it was: the coloured band round it is unmistakable because the colours are those of my old college and a rugger club I once played for combined with a light blue streak. That's why I bought it.

The black man's grin grew wider. 'That your briefcase too?' He gestured at my right hand.

'Of course it is,' I snapped. It seemed to me that the time had come for firmness. I didn't like the way they confronted me, their attitude.

'Good.' He drew the word out, like a croon. The lumber-jacketed man now managed a smile too, not a smile I liked at all. He gave the black man a quick look of what seemed to me like satisfaction and the black man spoke again. 'It was real kind of you to bring it along. Just as we hoped.'

'Eh?' Spines started to rise down the back of my neck. Cold sweat suddenly chilled my back.

The black man's face went menacing, savage. His half-beard now gave him a vicious look. 'Hand it over! And your wallet! Quick, man, quick! We got no time!'

Great hackles pricked up on my back, somewhere between my shoulder-blades. Blood started pumping at high pressure from a source within, suffusing my face and neck in high colour. Automatically I tightened my grip on the briefcase. 'Like hell I will! Give me my case! At once!'

His hand came out of his jacket, sweeping the six-inch blade of a polished steel knife into view. The smile snapped off, his teeth bared in rage. 'You hand it over right now, man, or you get hurt real bad. Real bad! Hand it over! Now! Now!'

I suppose that's how all muggers do it. The immediate intention of the shout is to terrify, with their all-too-real willingness to maim and kill. The victim freezes to the spot, obeys, paralysed out of the ability to run away like mad, hoping to extract something from the disaster, praying not to get hurt. The big lumber-jacketed man stepped forward at me, bringing his right hand out to beckon for my briefcase. To do so, his arm had to move across his body from right to left. It was a bad mistake because it made the arm inoperable from a fighting point of view and put his left completely out of the arena. Not that arms matter that much in a mêlée, human ones I mean. Any sportsman, and certainly any ex-rugby player, like me, knows that legs are much more powerful than arms and much more damaging, particularly when capped with good stout leather brogues with a thick,

11

solid leather sole and welt rather than the soft, tennis-type shoes he and the black man were wearing. I shifted my weight backwards and, still holding the briefcase, kicked him as hard as I could on the bone to the inside of the knee, beside the kneecap. I didn't dare go higher, much as I would have liked to, because a real stopper into the place where it hurts most, higher up, might have missed; I was out of practice and could have overbalanced, leaving the field clear for them to do me in on the ground.

He gave a yell of pain and stopped to grab the knee, giving me time to block a horrific knife-thrust from the black man with my briefcase, which fortunately is hard black fibreglass. Then I had to drop it and use both hands to deal with the next thrust. As the knife-wielder came back at me, I stepped away from him and turned, gathering his forearm in my left hand to deflect the knife. For a moment we were locked side by side in a grapple, so I took the precaution of standing on his canvas sports-shoe with the heel of my brogue, transferring my weight to it. He gasped and tried to break away, leaving enough space open for me to wallop him with my right in the best short hook I could muster. His foot was still pinned to the ground; it's an old booth-fighter's trick a Cambridge friend, who got his blue for boxing, taught me, and it's very effective. With any luck you tear the tendons in the arch of his foot as you smack him backwards, unable to break from you or to ride the punch.

I scored a bullseye, a beauty, right to the side of his jaw while he couldn't shift away. His eyes rolled and his knees buckled like rubber. The knife dropped and he went down on hands and knees, jerking his head so that the greasy cap fell off. At that point the lumber-jacketed one stopped hopping and hit me on the side of the head somewhere.

I went backwards in the direction of the rubber doors, my vision whirling the scene about me like a Catherine-wheel. The momentum took me through them helplessly, flailing my arms wildly out of balance, but I got one sight, one momentary flash-image that, together with the keen Great Lakes air outside, served to freeze my focus on to important events. The mediocre grey-suited man had now picked up both my suitcase and my briefcase and had come out through the doors, heading towards the roadworks and a narrow lane between them that led to the airport concourse with its taxis, limos and buses. He still used the same determined walk, not a run, just like someone preoccupied with getting to a flight on time would do, quite natural, quite unremarkable. I almost had a second to admire the professionalism of it as I regained my balance by whirling my arms like a windmill. Then I leapt after him with the maddened zeal of a man seeing his precious possessions disappearing, shaking my head to clear the numbness from the blow.

I used to be known, in my day as a front-row forward, for a rather accurate up-and-under punt kick of the type normally associated with stand-off halves and similar ilk, disconcerting from a forward expected to do nothing much more than shove, run and blunder. I used it now, with unrepentant fury, on the back of his right leg above the knee but below the buttock, where there are lots of important tendons and muscles and stringy bits that doctors advise you to look after. The toe of my shoe was travelling with maximum velocity and muscular propulsion as it sank into the back of his leg and kicked it forward, up and high into the air, like a can-can dancer. He went over backwards with gratifying promptness and a shriek, dropping the cases and half-falling on them as his back and head smacked the ground. That gave me a chance to jump on him and tread about a bit with both feet as I turned to meet the certain arrival of the big lumber-jacketed bloke, ignoring the squeals underfoot as I tried to refocus in the hard daylight.

It wasn't a promising situation. The suitcase-carrier was out of action and the black man was still evidently picking himself up, but my head was singing and I had a sudden onrush of reaction, of weakness, as you do after a clout. At that moment the lumber-jacket got to me. He had paused for long enough to pick up the black man's knife and, although he couldn't move as fast as he might, due to a painful knee, he came on at me in a ferocious bull-rush, swinging the horrid knife in a terrifying arc. The only encouraging prospect was that there were now, from behind me down the roadway, cries and shouts where it met the main concourse, even a screech of brakes. I jumped off the grey-suited professional and the knife missed, but I had to abandon my position near the cases. Mind you, the grey-suited one couldn't do much with them; he now had both hands clasped to the upper part of his right leg and was making tragically damaged noises. I dodged the knife again and managed to hit out, connecting without much force or impact to my assailant's body. It was a feeble blow and made no difference to the lumber-jacket; he crouched to leap once more.

Just then, the black man came out of the swing doors from the car park to rejoin the party, his eyes rolling as he lurched towards us. The lumber-jacket grinned, knowing that they now had me properly outnumbered. He dodged to the left of me, stuck out the knife and gestured to the black man to come in on the right as he aimed the point at my ribs. The black man caught his gesture, nodded, stepped forward, paused, and then collapsed in a heap on the tarmac.

The lumber-jacket was so surprised that he froze for an instant, gaping at the crumpled body on the floor. I didn't bother to explain to him that the effects of concussion can be very unpredictable, as any rugger man knows, because the sight had given me a great, joyous, resurgent spurt of energy. I went in past the outstretched knife with one terrific right to his face and then I was all over him, it was no time to hesitate or let up, he'd kill me, so I let him have it, left, right, left, face, stomach, face again, neck, jaw, nose –

'Freeze! Police! Freeze!'

I hardly heard the shout. I had the lumber-jacketed man against the nearest wall now, I was battle-crazy, mad, head down, pistoning in punches like a maniac, I was going to kill the bastard, murder him, hack the knife-wielding assassin to the ground, stamp on him like a –

'I said freeze! Freeze or I fire! Police! Police!'

At this point I heard it. The shout had become a bellow and made me turn my head. More strident voices penetrated my hearing. Near me, pistol held in both hands, was a policeman, youngish-looking, legs astride and braced, like a well-trained man. The barrel of the gun was pointed straight at my eye. Behind him, flashing lights whirled on a police patrol car skewed across the construction site. Behind that, another car was screeching to a halt, siren wailing, lights rotating. His finger whitened on the trigger. I stepped back.

'Don't move! Don't move!'

'I – um – I – er, this, these men – '

'I said don't move! Stay where you are!' The pistol jerked. Staring straight at it, straight down the barrel, it seemed to me, I had the sudden impression that he was going to fire right into my eye. It was a horrible moment, a split fraction of a second when, if I had been drowning, my life with all its sins might have passed before me. Guiltily I watched the lumber-jacket slide down the wall with a moan. The knife clattered on the ground somewhere. Two more policemen, burly in black uniforms, ran up alongside the young one and I sensed, rather than saw, his muscles relax as the shakes started to come over me. Ignoring his instruction, I took a step or two away so as to be able to lean against a barrier for support. Behind the eyes I closed for a moment, in the darkness of my mind, the reproachful face of Jeremy White began to float before me. That the events of the last two weeks should lead to this, I could imagine him groaning; is there nothing that can be done to keep Tim Simpson out of trouble?

Chapter Two

If I had not been out of my office for a few days, doing the Bank's business elsewhere, Jeremy might not have got so steamed up about things. As it was, the report had been with him for that time without any explanation from me and, always the case with Jeremy White, he let his natural instincts run amok for a bit until he heard that I was back. He sent for me right away – it was about a week or two before my trip to Chicago – and was braying at me the minute I sat down, that sunny September afternoon, there in his office at the Bank. It's not a bad office as the Bank's offices go, oak-panelled but light, reasonably light anyway, decorated with one of Whistler's paintings of Wapping, all ships and spars and tangle above the models' heads, and another painting I admire, one of a three-masted White timber ship en route from Manaos in the mid-nineteenth century. The Whites founded their business by importing rosewood from Brazil but White's Bank is into many other things now, like stocks and bonds and corporate finance, quite apart from its overseas operations.

'Tim! This is horrific! Christerby's are going to make a complete cock of things!'

'I take it,' I said calmly, accepting a cup of coffee from his secretary, who winked at me knowingly before leaving the room, 'that you have received my interim management report on the state of the art – to coin a phrase – at the rooms?'

He glared at me. 'I have indeed! This is no time for

17

flippancy, damn it! What on earth is that man Howarth thinking of? The business is still losing a fortune on its New York auctions and he's talking of an acquisition or even a green-fields branch in Chicago!' He waved a sheaf of papers at me. 'This report of yours should be pepped up and circulated to the entire board! What does Charles Massenaux think? Hey?'

It should perhaps be explained that White's Bank own a thirty-per-cent stake in the shares of Christerby's, International Fine Art Auctioneers, an investment made possible a while back through the happy intervention of my old friend Charles Massenaux, the head of the Impressionist department and now a director of the firm. To keep a watching brief on behalf of White's, I was on the Christerby's board as a non-executive director. This fitted in well with the responsibility I had for looking after White's Art Investment Fund, an invention of Jeremy's and mine intended as a service to those clients of ours who wished to invest in art without actually buying a Rembrandt themselves.

The man Howarth Jeremy was referring to was the presiding managing director of Christerby's International, a man not originally an auctioneer, but a supposedly proven international businessman and marketer, very acceptable to the financial institutions who had invested in Christerby's and, apparently, to its public shareholders. Like its competitors, Christerby's was heavily committed to developing its US business and started with a great fanfare in New York, where some record prices had been achieved. Alas, like one or two of its competitors, Christerby's had found the costs to be astronomic and was not yet showing a profit on its substantial investment over there.

'Charles,' I said, sipping my coffee, 'is an expert on Impressionist paintings, sculpture and various other subjects. He is an extremely competent director of the British company. But he is no expert on marketing in the USA, even if he does have a sound knowledge of the relevant collections our American friends have amassed.'

Jeremy gave an impatient wave. 'Really, Tim! Stop flannelling! What does he think?'

'He doesn't like it.'

'There you are! Neither do I!'

I put my coffee down. 'Jeremy, whatever you may think about Howarth's intentions, the USA holds the key to much of the future for fine art auctioneers. The overall business, right now, is comfortably profitable –'

'Only because of London and Europe!'

I ignored his interruption. 'The overall business is profitable despite losses in New York, which can be regarded as an investment for the future. In due time New York will be organized on a profitable basis, but Howarth's contention is that if he waits until then before expanding and establishing the business in other American centres such as Chicago and Los Angeles, his competitors may have got in ahead and pre-empted his expansion. Ergo, he is looking to do it now.'

'Madness! Throwing good money after bad!'

'Jeremy,' I said patiently, but with an effort because I'd had a busy week with quite enough to endure already, 'Jeremy, it is perfectly reasonable for the chief executive of the company to look at such expansionary options before deciding on where next to allocate his resources.'

'Now you're waffling. Like a management consultant or something.'

I gritted my teeth. 'I am a management consultant. Was a management consultant. When you met me. You found such things useful once.'

He shot me an amused look. Jeremy is a peremptory devil but he and I get on well most of the time. When I had first met him, Jeremy was still very much the junior member of a cadet branch of the White family, running his own little outfit in personal finance in Park Lane. With his natural flair for money-making, tax avoidance and publicity, plus a certain amount of assistance from me and others, he was now a full board member of White's Bank in the City of London. At the beginning, things had been very different; he was then struggling to establish himself and needed more expertise behind him than his own entrepreneurial qualities could muster. I had been sold into his office to organize his chaotic administration and to recruit an accountant or finance director for him. When I finished this task, he suddenly offered me a job. Jeremy and I had much in common on art and antiques, had mooted the idea of an Art Fund together, and he was obviously a high-flier. I had not been long divorced from Carol, my ex, and was not very inspired by the worthy firm of consultants I worked for. I joined Jeremy with cheerful abandon, thinking that I might as well have a bit of fun for a couple of years. Now here we were, nearly four years later, becoming gravid and respectable and serious; it seemed extraordinary. Jeremy still retained his energy, his blond imperious looks, his sudden Etonian arpeggios of hilarious laughter, but he had responsibilities now, much bigger responsibilities. Conservatism was setting in.

The telephone rang. Jeremy picked it up with a quick grab of his yachtsman's hand. 'Yes, Clara? Oh, splendid, Andy Casey. By all means put him through.'

I looked at him in surprise. On the whole it was I who tended to deal with Andy Casey since I had charge of overseas matters, but there was no reason why he and Jeremy shouldn't be in direct contact. Jeremy clamped his hand over the mouthpiece.

'I asked him to phone,' he said. 'So that you and he can arrange your visit.'

I gaped at him. 'My visit? What visit?'

'My dear Tim! To Chicago, of course. We can't have this man Howarth splashing our money out on wildcat projects without checking the facts ourselves. You must go there. And to New York. Find out what on earth they're intending to do.'

My jaw dropped. 'For Christ's sake, Jeremy! I'm not an executive director of Christerby's! Even if I were, this would be an unwarranted intrusion. Howarth might be furious.'

'Of course not! If he wants to expand into Chicago he'll want finance. Our arrangement with Owens, McLeod and Casey exists to handle that sort of thing. It's quite in order for us to see them locally.'

My jaw dropped even further. 'Howarth can arrange finance from where he likes. He doesn't have to use us or our contacts just because we're shareholders.'

I got a full view of the whites of Jeremy's eyes as they flared open. 'Oh yes he does! We exist for the purpose of financing such things. Let him try for finance elsewhere at his peril.'

There's no dealing with Jeremy when he's in one of these moods, so I waved at the telephone. 'You'd

21

better say hello to Andy. He is in Chicago, waiting patiently, I suppose?'

He scowled, but unclasped his hand from the receiver. 'Andy? Jeremy here. Hello there! How are you? Splendid, splendid. Tim is bursting to speak to you, so I'll hand him over. Mine to your lot too, thanks. Fine, fine. Here's Tim.'

The look I gave him as I took the instrument was entirely lost on him. He picked up his sheaf of papers and avoided my stare. It meant that my trip to Chicago could not be avoided. Jeremy's decisions on such matters amounted to commands; argument would be useless. To Chicago I would have to go, willy-nilly. Andy's pleasant tones sounded in my ear, turning my irritated mind from the maddening prospect of Jeremy. 'Tim? Hi! How's Sue? Great. Are you going to bring her over with you? Or has she done the wise thing and left you at last?'

'No,' I said firmly, in answer to both questions. 'No, I'm not. Bringing her with me. I'm afraid that this will have to be a short business trip. I gather that Jeremy has talked to you about Christerby's business plans?'

'Nope. Just that you wanted to fix a visit to see me about something they want to finance. I'm all ears, Tim. What's it about?'

How bloody typical, I thought, how absolutely in character, Jeremy as usual, firing from the hip, leaving the 'detail' to someone else, poking his nose into everything but leaving the slog to me. 'It's quite an interesting one, Andy. Christerby's look like setting up a Chicago branch, either from grass roots or by acquisition. I will have to look at the idea pretty thoroughly.'

There was a momentary silence before the voice at

the other end spoke. 'Set up a branch? Here in Chicago? You mean a full-blown auction house?'

'Yes. That's what they're looking at.'

'Wow! I thought they were still taking a tough ride over in New York?'

'They are. But Howarth doesn't want to wait for that to come right before getting his network established.'

Another brief silence. 'Well, I'll be glad to give any help I can. It'll certainly cost money. I guess we'll be involved in the action, if it goes?'

'That's the idea. I need to see you and then maybe we'd go to New York to talk to them there. I know that there are already one or two good auction houses in Chicago and we can talk about them. Maybe even talk to them as well.'

'OK. When are you coming over?'

We exchanged dates and I promised to telex him my exact plans. I knew Andy Casey well enough to understand his somewhat noncommittal mid-West conversation. Emotional backchat is not the style of your Chicagoan banker; the English are positively garrulous compared with them.

We were just about finished and I was moving the receiver back towards its cradle when I heard Andy call out and put the instrument back to my ear.

'Hey, Tim! I almost forgot! You're just the guy!'

'Yes, Andy?'

'Have you ever heard of an Englishman called Frewen?'

'Frewen?'

'Yes. Frewen.' He spelt it out.

I frowned in thought. 'No, can't say I have. In connection with what? When? To do with banking, or art, is this?'

There was a chuckle from the other end. 'Neither. This is to do with old gold-mine shares, Tim. He was once a rancher, I'm told, Wyoming area. About a hundred years ago.'

I chuckled back. 'Can't say it rings a bell, Andy. Before my time. I'm not much up on gold-mining, or cowboys. They're a strictly American zone. We never had a Deadwood stage.'

'Sussex family,' said Jeremy suddenly, still scowling at his sheaf of papers. 'Very old. Hunting.'

'Jeremy?'

'Frewen,' he muttered, turning the papers with another scowl. 'Sussex.'

I gave him a look, which he didn't see, and spoke back to the telephone. 'Andy? Jeremy says it's an old Sussex family. If that's any use?'

'Mortal ruin.' Jeremy's voice was thick and his head shook. His face was congested over the papers attached to my report. I clapped my hand over the receiver. I'd had enough of this.

'Now see here, Jeremy, it's quite bloody unnecessary to exaggerate like this! Mortal ruin indeed! Damn that! Christerby's are in good shape overall. New York will probably come right soon and you're taking a ridiculously pessimistic attitude, to my mind. Nothing venture, nothing gain. Where's the merchant adventurer spirit, eh? That sort of hyperbole is quite offensive, especially when my report points out –'

My voice trailed off. He was staring at me in a way that, together with an imperious gathering of his pose, stopped me. His face set in disbelief. 'My dear Tim! This really won't do. You're becoming obsessive. It's not like you to become so defensive about a thing like this.' He waved the sheaf of papers. 'I was talking about Moreton Frewen, my dear chap, not these.

Mortal ruin.' He grinned wolfishly. 'It's a pun, my dear boy. Mortal Frewen. Moreton Ruin. Get it?'

I held the telephone still. Valuable seconds passed. 'Jeremy,' I said feebly, at last, my voice croaking a bit, 'what on earth are you talking about?'

'Moreton Frewen of course! Who else? Andy was asking about him, wasn't he? Frewen was known in the City as Mortal Ruin. All his backers always lost their money. On every scheme he ever had. Ask my cousin Donald. His father lost his shirt on a couple of Frewen's crazy investments. Some time ago, mind, but bankers have long memories, you know. My dear Tim, I do sometimes worry about you nowadays. You don't really seem to have quite the same *grasp* that you used to have.'

I managed to get my hand off the telephone receiver. One of the amazing things about Jeremy is that you never can tell what his mind is going to come up with next. It's stocked with the sort of esoteric knowledge that people claim mine is cluttered with. 'Andy? Are you still there? Was this man called Moreton Frewen?'

His voice came back sharply, interested and keen. 'That's it! Moreton Frewen. Does Jeremy know something?'

'Jeremy says he was known as Mortal Ruin in the City of London because everyone lost money on his schemes. Does that help?'

There was a laugh from the other end. 'Mortal Ruin, eh? That figures. It's no great shakes, Tim, but we handle a certain amount of our older clients' trustee business. One of them came into a pile of old stock certificates, shares you'd call them, some in a gold-mining company that had mines in Utah and Colorado. It was some kind of share swap deal originally, I guess, because this guy says that Frewen must have taken them in exchange. He probably left them with a security company of some sort at one time for safekeeping, because they've got writing on the envelope they're in. Something about keeping them with the sergeant for safety. Our client isn't too excited though, fortunately. Most of those mines were worked out years ago, if they ever had much gold in them to start with. There are other shares relating to South Dakota, too, I'll tell you, since you brought up the Deadwood stage.'

'Oh really? You said that Frewen was a rancher in Wyoming. Didn't leave any cattle ranges to your client, did he? They might still be worth something.'

Another laugh came down the line. 'Heck, no. Frewen pulled out of Wyoming way before this gold-mine thing. A lot of Britishers invested in cattle in the 1870s and 1880s, Tim, that's history from Chicago down to Texas. Most of them lost their pants as well as their shirts. The ranges got overstocked and a few bad winters wrecked the grazing. That and the rustlers and the settlers coming in; led to the Johnson County War, I seem to recall, but I never did listen to my history lessons much.'

'You've lost me. And this call is costing you a fortune. Is that all you needed? It sounds as though the certificates might have more value as collector's items.'

There was a pause. 'Oh – well – I guess – look, if it's no trouble, just to please the client. He is one of our best investors. Anything else that you can find. Find easily, I mean. Don't take a lot of trouble.'

'OK, Andy. 'Bye now.'

' 'Bye, Tim.'

I put the phone down. Jeremy was still frowning.

'You seem in no hurry to leave,' he said peevishly. 'Can't you go to Chicago before next week?'

'No I can't! There's the Christerby's board meeting. I must attend.'

'Oh yes, of course. It'll be as well for Howarth to know that we're doing some reconnoitring for him.'

'Jeremy, really. I shall have to tell him that I'm going to be in the States on other business anyway and will simply take soundings at OMC.'

'OMC?'

I sighed. 'Owens, McLeod and Casey.'

'Ah. I do detest these cryptic initials. What business will you ostensibly be visiting for?'

'Oh God, I'll think of something. The Brazilian railway project. Gold-mining in Utah. Cattle in Wyoming. Something.'

Jeremy laughed. 'You sound much like Frewen yourself when you talk of schemes like that. No one'll believe you. You really must come to Donald's garden party on Sunday if this weather holds. It'll be the last of the season. He gives a good binge.'

'I really don't think' I said cautiously, 'that Donald altogether appreciates our presence, Jeremy, even if he is an expert on this Frewen bloke. We came in here, after all, when Donald got the push – early retirement, I mean – from your Uncle Richard, two years ago. I rather think that Donald will regard us as the Troops of Midian or something. I know that he's sixty-six but he wouldn't have retired for years yet if there hadn't been a Night of the Long Knives here at the Bank. We'd still be in Park Lane.'

'Nonsense! Enjoys his retirement. On the Hamble nearly every day of the week. Sails in fair weather and foul. Says it's the best thing that ever happened to him. He'll tell you about Frewen all right; his father used to rant on for hours about him. Besides, it's a good party and Mary is counting on your bringing Sue; she wants to see her.'

'I had no idea that White's were involved with this Frewen man.'

'Oh, they weren't really. Just Donald's father. An investment thing. More like greed, actually. Served 'em right. Frewen was very well connected, of course.'

'Was he? How?'

He scowled at the papers again impatiently. 'Frightfully. Knew all the best people. They were once big landowners. Sussex and Leicester and Ireland. Good county stock; Moreton Frewen was a great horseman. Superb hunter.'

'Oh. County stock. Horses.'

He gave me another of his looks. 'There's no need to curl your lip. He was Winston Churchill's uncle, after all.'

'You – you – you mean Sir Winston Churchill? *The* Winston Churchill?'

'Well, who else do you think I meant? I realize you were only a little lad at the time, or whatever, out on the pampas or at your prep school perhaps, but we did have a prime minister here, in the 'fifties, who, during the war, was – '

I left the room. There's simply no dealing with Jeremy when he's in one of those moods.

Chapter Three

The drive down to Haslemere was glorious. In case you had forgotten, summer last year was not exactly the greatest, but they tried to make up for it a bit in the early autumn, when the weather went into that sunny, misty, hop-gathering mood that makes England worth living in for its brief duration. London, especially our Brompton area, had a nostalgic glow over it. The countryside, on the way to Donald White's, down the Portsmouth Road and on over the Devil's Punchbowl, spread green and golden swoops of rolling mature fields and woods around us to emphasize, after an absence, that the Home Counties were still here and safe, beautiful and welcoming.

Sue hummed quietly as I drove the Jaguar moderately through this amiable landscape. She likes a trip out on a Sunday from time to time, even though Sue, like me, is a city dweller, preoccupied by city pursuits and art galleries. She works at the Tate, where she is what is known as a Curator, recently promoted to category D, whatever that may mean in the Civil Service apart from more money, which she was rather pleased to get. She was at Oxford, I regret to say, although I don't hold it against her, and then at the Courtauld. She is highly qualified in art history and various other aspects of the subject which I frequently find very useful, and she spends a lot of time immured in a sort of basement below the Tate, where they do research and cataloguing and muttering about special displays and so forth. They claim that you have to have considerable managerial, organizational and planning abilities to be a Curator, of any letter in the alphabet, and I rather incline to agree with them, because Sue certainly has all those. She's not exactly bossy, you understand, but she's rather crisp and headgirlish from time to time, exuding a sort of teacher-type quality of feminist confidence which can be disconcerting. Women will say that it is only disconcerting to a chap like me, whatever that may mean, but all I can say is that with a girl like Sue you can never take anything for granted, including her attitude to us, me and she I mean, which is modern to say the least.

I have actually been married once, fairly disastrously, and after the divorce Carol, my ex, went to live in New Zealand, which is about as far away as you can get and still only need to speak English. Sue and I have been together off and on for about three years, interspersed with a long year that she spent in Australia on an exchange with another gallery. You may well ask why the ladies of my close companionship evince a desire to rush off to the Antipodes and I'm not answering that; all I can say is that I missed her horribly, so I suppose that I'm more than a bit keen on Sue. She, however, takes the view that either I'm not yet to be trusted, or considered serious and responsible enough for marriage, or she herself is not yet ready for it, despite having reached her late twenties. I'm not sure which is the prevailing theory; it rather depends on what sort of mood she's in. All I know is that despite this she is a terrific girl, as passionate as could be asked for under the professional, businesslike exterior, and that the last fairly settled year or so while we have been living together has been great. I'm afraid that Sue has been a bit close to danger once or twice because of various unpleasantnesses that have happened in pursuit of works of art for White's Fund, but she's been very good about it and, no question of it, has contributed a good deal of intelligence to the proceedings.

That morning she was wearing a rather smart outfit consisting of a suit of light tweed that looked very simple but that I therefore suspect was rather expensive, and a blouse and some matching shoes and handbag. The handbag replaced Sue's usual daily satchel-like bag which she normally carries slung over one shoulder and which contains all her indispensable accessories, so I wondered how she would get through the day on her current smart but minimal equipment.

'Isn't Donald very old?' she asked, breaking a long silence that had taken in a sweep of hills around Hindhead.

'Not really. Well, he's sixty-six, if you want to be accurate. Retired.'

'Ah. I thought you and Jeremy weren't exactly his favourite people. Didn't he have to retire when Sir Richard agreed to having Jeremy on the board?'

'Yes, he did. But, to be fair, that happened before we joined.'

'The events were connected though, weren't they?'

'Er, yes. Sort of. The Bank was starting to lose a lot of money and some of the big shareholders wanted a change. Jeremy was acceptable to them. Should think so too. But he says that Donald doesn't bear a grudge. Spends all his time sailing from the Hamble. Sees quite a lot of Jeremy now for that reason.'

'I thought he had a tin leg or something.'

'He has. Lost a leg in the war. It doesn't stop him

from sailing. He's quite nimble, I believe. Remarkable man that way.'

She shot me a glance. 'But not the business way?'

'No. Donald was part of the old guard who didn't understand what has happened to merchant banking and didn't like what they could understand. They hated our Park Lane operation. It's all history now, though. Thanks to Jeremy and a lot of work, we are at least decently profitable again. I shan't be drawing the dole just yet.'

'I'm glad to hear it. Hadn't fancied keeping you, Tim. Oh, what a nice house.'

We had turned off a side road into the entrance to Donald White's establishment. The drive led down the side of an open field with a three-bar fence beyond which a bay hunter grazed peacefully near a copse. The house itself was not large, but it was of mellow brick with white Georgian window frames and looked settled, cheerful and well-kept. I put it down mentally as eighteenth-century, a farmhouse, and the outbuildings beside it, which included a stable block, looked as though they belonged to the same period. It wasn't large, any of it, but it was very useful, well-planned, the sort of place a country man would be able to run without too much assistance or outside help. As we drew up I saw people clustered on a terrace behind the house, talking animatedly. Jeremy waved as we got out of the car and came bounding towards us.

'Sue! Tim! Splendid! Donald's asked me to bring you over. Mary'll be tickled pink that you're here, says she needs Sue to talk to. Haven't seen you for ages, Sue. You look absolutely gorgeous.'

She smiled and gave him a friendly kiss before we walked over to join the others. Jeremy married Mary

Waller, as she then was, just after the big shake-up at the Bank. Mary was once Sir Richard White's secretary and knew the inner workings of the Bank like nobody else, so that in a way Jeremy stole a march on everyone when he joined the board. They'd been hoping to defeat him by his ignorance, but, with Mary's inside track, Jeremy had out-matched them all. Let me hasten to say that the move was not just a political expedient; Jeremy was madly keen on Mary well before that and she's devoted to him. It has been a very successful marriage, and Mary retired from the Bank to produce two children in fairly short order, so she's now *hors de combat*, as you might say. I have a sneaking feeling that she might return to the Bank one day, and it occurred to me that she would be glad to have Sue there that morning because Donald was part of her old days, when she sat outside Sir Richard's office, and was one of the Bank's secretaries, rather than a full-blown member of the family. She waved to us cheerfully, embraced Sue happily, kissed me with considerable warmth and then we went across to pay our dues to Donald.

I remembered his face quite clearly. I never had any direct dealings with him because by the time Jeremy had brought me in to the Bank from Park Lane the bloodbath was over and Donald had gone. Once or twice later, while we were wrestling with Sir Richard, trying to make sense of what he, the Chairman was doing, I had seen Donald around the Bank clearing up his papers, attending a pension fund meeting, that sort of thing. Then I lost sight of him. There was no reason for me to deal with him, he wasn't involved in the Art Fund at all; in fact, like Sir Richard, he disapproved of it, so I didn't see him again. The battle with Sir Richard had gone our way and now he had left as well, so that I had no contact with the older generation of White's and, frankly, hadn't had much desire to have it.

Donald White was a tall man, weatherbeaten and crinkly-brown of face, with sharp blue eyes and bright white hair, still fairly thick. He wore a navy-blue blazer of nautical cut, grey flannels and brown suede brogues. A dark marine-looking cravat filled the open neck of his spotless white shirt. He looked fit and active, as a yachtsman might. The first image that came to my mind was of someone impersonating the late David Niven. It was only when Donald stepped forward to shake hands with Sue that I noticed the slight drag of the leg, the stiffness of movement.

'How d'you do?' His smile at Sue was gallant and the eyes crinkled and twinkled with great charm. 'Sue, is it? What a pleasure. Ah, and this is the legendary Tim Simpson, I know. We have met before, I think? At the Bank? But alas, only briefly, eh?'

'I'm afraid so. This is very pleasant.' I tried to hide my embarrassment at the glancing reference to his departure. 'It's very kind of you to invite us down here. What a delightful place.'

'Glad you like it. It does rather suit me.' His smile was open and friendly. Sue was being led away by Mary to a table with a sherry on it. 'Gin and tonic?'

'Thank you.' A man in a white coat appeared with a tray of sizeable glasses, sizeably filled. I took one.

'Jeremy says you'd like to talk to me about one of my father's little *bête-noires*, old Moreton Frewen?' He grinned inquisitively. 'Thought we'd heard the last of him many years ago.'

I smiled back. 'Well, it was just an odd coincidence. Came up from Owens, McLeod and Casey. Some

34

gold shares, gold-mine shares, that had once belonged to him. In Chicago. Jeremy seemed to think that you'd know something about him. Said he was called Mortal Ruin in the City.'

Donald laughed then, a full-blooded laugh that brought one or two more people to our side. He introduced them briefly and chuckled at me again, beckoning Jeremy to him as he spoke. 'You're absolutely right! Absolutely! He was a menace. My father always called him that. I should explain to you – I was born in 1920. Frewen was still alive then, of course, but only just. My father, as it happened, married twice, d'you see; first wife died. My mother was his second. Father was over fifty when I was born. He got involved in a few of Frewen's schemes around the turn of the century, when he first went into the thick of business. My God, there were some frightful projects! A Hoffman engine, vitrified bricks, incessant silver-mines. Frewen was a fanatical bimetallist, of course. Gold came into it from time to time. There was a fluid called Electrozones. Disgusting stuff. Oddly enough – it was a sort of disinfectant – my dear old pa did quite well out of that later, when someone else took it over and called it Milton or something like that.'

'Milton? I thought that was a baby-bottle disinfectant.'

'It is. Moreton Frewen didn't always stick to gold, silver and ranching. But he lost out on Electrozones, and so did Horatio Bottomley, who collaborated in promoting it. My father had a lot to say about that. He became a dedicated disliker of Moreton Frewen. Ha! My goodness! I haven't heard that name for ages.'

'Oh dear. I hope I haven't raised old skeletons?'

'Oh no. Well, not really. How on earth did he come up after all these years?'

I took a refreshing draught of gin and tonic. 'From Chicago, as I said. Andy Casey asked about him.'

'Chicago? Chicago? Not very appropriate, surely? Frewen was anathema to Chicago. Tried to cut 'em out. What connection is that? If it's not confidential, of course.'

'Oh no, it's no secret. The old gold-mine shares are for mines in Utah and South Dakota. Colorado as well. A client of Andy's has come by them somehow.'

'Really?' Donald's delight was evident, conveying itself to the small group who had clustered around us. 'I love that sort of thing. Deadwood and the Homestake and all that. Wonderful. Were they Frewen's?'

'It seems so. They have his writing across them. Apparently he lodged them with a protection outfit, a security company of some kind. It says to keep them with the sergeant, written in what they think is Frewen's writing. Andy was looking for clues to their history, to help his client.'

Donald White laughed. 'Wild West stuff, young Tim! The Deadwood stage! Do you know that Frewen took his bride, Clara Jerome, out to his ranch in Wyoming on the Deadwood stage? Eh? And brought her back pregnant in it. Lost the child, I'm afraid. But there was an extraordinary sequel: Buffalo Bill Cody brought that stage to London when my father was in his thirties and used it in his show at Earls Court. My father went to see it. The cowboys recognized Frewen in the audience and got him to drive the stage round the arena. Extraordinary. Cody admired Frewen enormously, thought him a hell of a chap. They'd hunted together in Wyoming. Great excitement, there was. I've often thought that my father threw money into Frewen's schemes on the thrill of that Wild West Show. That and Frewen's tongue, of course. He could charm the snake out of a tree, Frewen could.'

'Oh dear. Did your father lose everything he put into them?'

'No, not everything. That was always the queer thing about Frewen. He wasn't a crook. Some of his backers made money. Most of them lost. Nowadays he'd have been a promoter, a PR man – even a merchant banker – no, not that; he couldn't be trusted with money. He didn't steal or anything but he had no business cool. It was bad luck on him in Wyoming; he was a great country man, that he understood perfectly, but no financier.'

There was silence. Donald looked reflectively into his glass. I cleared my throat. 'Well, thanks for all that fascinating background. I don't suppose it'll make the shares valuable. But I love that sort of history; it brings things to life. The dry documents, I mean. Gives them life.'

He grinned. 'I feel the same. Kept with a sergeant, you say?'

'Yes.'

'Hm. Frewen wasn't military. His younger brother was. But the Frewens were landed gentry in those days. Great horsemen. Hunting. Foxes, of course.'

My eye turned automatically at this towards the railed paddock where the bay paraded himself proudly on the green turf. Mary and Sue were headed irrevocably in that direction, talking animatedly. My stare after them drew an amused look from Donald, who nudged my arm confidentially.

'Don't let an old buffer's reminiscences detain you, my boy. Splendid girl. Wish I were your age. Go on, do your duty and join them. We can talk later. I've got to circulate over there with some locals. We'll catch up with each other, I've no doubt. Keep your glass filled by the way; I'll leave you to look after yourself.'

He turned off towards another group, leaving me decided that I liked Donald and that he was of the right material. I watched him greet a man in a tweed plaid suit and turned away myself, noting how Mary and Sue were changing their tones as they approached the horse.

'Oh! Isn't he beautiful? Come on boy! Over here – have you got a lump of sugar?'

I shook my head sadly and ambled after them. Most of Donald's guests seemed to be prosperously-retired locals with a distinctly country flavour, rapt in conversations about winter barley and four-wheel-drive vehicles. There were a couple of yachtsmen and a stockbroker I knew vaguely, all clustered with Jeremy, who was holding forth about marine insurance. I decided that I could do a lot worse than join the ladies.

We stood at the pasture fence in the splendid sunshine, Mary and Sue making a fuss of the big hunter, who lapped it up, nuzzling them this way and that over the rough top rail. He was a stallion, which excited them; it's funny how girls, particularly English girls, have this thing about great powerful bone-headed brutes like horses. In my youth in South America I used to ride a bit, in comfort on a big saddle with a sheepskin under it, holding the reins in one hand, not two, but I never liked it that much. Here in England they have these mad girls perched on arse-cracking saddles and they hold the reins in two hands, so that you can't do anything useful once you're on the horse but ride it. It's a strange business. I gave the brute a leer and he grinned at me knowingly, pulling his big soft upper lip back to show his huge yellow choppers in a parodic reply, as though to say, 'If you don't pull one or both of these prize women, I'll have them for myself.' Disgusting. A man's horse, I realized, definitely a man's horse, no question.

After a while Jeremy excused himself from a group and came across to us. He grimaced at the horse. Jeremy is a yachtsman first and foremost; horses are not his style.

'Donald's always been keen on the gee-gees,' he said, relegating the fine animal to an amorphous category of hack. 'Before the war when his lot lived up in the East Midlands he used to ride a heck of a lot, apparently. To hounds and all that. Point-to-points. You name it.'

'He must have been pretty young.'

Jeremy glanced at me. 'Nineteen when the war broke out. Joined up right away. Cavalryman. Dashing stuff.'

'Not the Navy?' I swung in surprise to look at the blue-blazered figure, so neat and nautical, well away from us in a group towards the house.

'No, no. Donald's no naval man. Took up sailing much later. Armoured cars for him. He was in the 16th Lancers.'

I glanced back from the house, feeling rather than thinking the line that without much reason or relevance came into my head. 'I 'listed at home for a lancer,' I murmured, half to myself, half to the horse, who was still leering at me a bit in that aggressive way that horses have, rolling an eye without having the faintest idea what he was at.

'Oh, who would not sleep with the brave?'

She's quick, is Sue. She shot the next line of the verse at me with an impish grin from close by, on my left, yet with a reflective smile replacing the first, meaningful flick of her eyelashes, as though she was sharing a long-held secret with me, partly suggestive and provocative, but also private, knowing that the sleep referred to was death, not what you might think. Her eyes shone and she squeezed my arm gently from her place close by, in a movement that I was sure Mary White noticed and which still, after all this time, turned my heart over in a way that no other girl but Sue has ever done. I winked back at her in complicity, and was about to continue the verse, when Jeremy's voice spoke behind me, making me jump.

'A. E. Housman,' he boomed, with a satisfied smile. 'Sort of poet you can't resist when you're in your late teens.'

The disconcerting thing about Jeremy, although why it should be I can't really justify, is this sort of occasional burst into literate utterance. He is, after all, highly educated. I mean, even Eton and Oxford have to have a civilizing effect of some kind on a man, but I suppose that because his exterior persona nowadays is so City, so banker, radiating High City folklore and deals, financial jargon and Stock Exchange gossip, I tend to forget that underneath that aggressively business-besotted surface there is a well-rounded individual with a common cultural experience. I gave him a congratulatory bow for the accuracy of his identification but he was staring into his empty glass for a moment.

'Get you all another?' he queried, looking up. 'Mary? Sue? Tim? Another g-and-t?'

The girls refused and turned back to lavish their affections on the horse, so I offered to keep Jeremy company and strolled towards the white-coated waiter with him, feeling Mary's oddly disconcerted glance on my back for a fleeting moment as I turned to go.

'He lost his leg in North Africa,' Jeremy's voice was quiet. 'Chasing Rommel. He was twenty-two. It was a bad wound. Long time before they found him and his armoured car. All the others were dead. It took a lot of healing. He couldn't ever ride properly to hounds again. He tried for years and nearly killed himself with falls. The doctors got him to stop in the end and he just canters for pleasure now. Anyway, that's why he took up sailing and moved down here. It's only thirty miles to the Solent and he's got the pick of the places – the Hamble, Chichester, wherever. While he was laid up recovering from the wound, back in England during the war, he had a lot of time at home. He and his father got very close, then. He heard all the old man's stories – he was born in 1870. Probably did both of them a lot of good to have so much time together, with a big age difference like that, I mean. Anyway, that's how he knows all this Frewen stuff. His father was a bit obsessive about it.'

'Did he ever marry? Donald, I mean.'

'Oh yes. French, she was. Agnes, of all names. Nurse here during the war. They sailed everywhere together. No children, though. She was charming and adored him, but she died of cancer four years ago. He's had some bad luck, I'm afraid, has Donald. But he's made of the right stuff; doesn't show it. I'm glad I've come to know him much better. Through sailing, I mean.'

'Does he miss the Bank?'

'He did. Badly. Doesn't now, though. Like many retired men, I find, Tim, even the dedicated ones. Once you break the habit, somehow work doesn't seem that important.'

'I'm looking forward to that.'

He grinned. 'I don't believe you and don't try to convince me. You have a low boredom threshold, like me. Come on; we'd better join the throng again.'

We replenished our glasses and moved into the gathering, which was composed of couples, most of them older than me. I was promptly buttonholed by a stoutish matron in a woollen outfit which clung to her with rather more affection than she might have liked, but who turned out to be a sporting old girl whose son played full-back for his college. She displayed a remarkable degree of technical knowledge about rugger and claimed to have seen me at Twickenham in my halcyon years.

'You've weathered jolly well,' she bellowed flatteringly. 'I always thought that front row men went frightfully to pot once they stopped playing. D'you take exercise of some sort?'

'Er, not really. Try to keep off the beer as much as possible.'

'Don't jog, or anything?'

'Good God, no!'

'Wise man. They drop like cocks from heart failure round here once they try that. My husband – that's him over there, going gently purple – played for the Army for a long time but, thank God, never tried anything except golf once he stopped rugby.'

I decided not to point out that a reasonably youthful cove like me could hardly be compared to the splendid old johnny with flowing curves whom she had indicated, but decided it wasn't worth it. It probably wouldn't have shocked her if I'd said that Sue kept me pretty fit too, but the old dear was off on the subject of the Stock Exchange by then, and had got the bit thoroughly between her teeth on that topic. She was remarkably shrewd, and obviously loved playing the market, so we got into animated conversation on the latest scandals – financial ones, I mean – until, all of a sudden, I realized that we were practically the only people left at the party and that Sue, Mary and Jeremy were regarding me with great good humour, waiting to go. I made my excuses and separated from the old dear.

'Didn't know you went in for generals' wives,' murmured Jeremy, as I joined the three of them.

'Now Jeremy, really – generals? Her husband? The puce old josser in the ginger suit?'

'Major-General McIntyre. Medical Corps. Has kept an eye on Donald for many years, when not in the Far East. Looks as though he's fuelled entirely on Singapore Slings, doesn't he?'

I chuckled. 'He certainly does. I don't know how good he is at mending broken bones, but I can tell you that his wife's hot stuff on the stock market, Jeremy. We should offer her a job in our broking department.'

An expression of pain crossed his face. Jeremy has always wanted White's to pep up their act in the broking world, long before the Big Bang, but older directors got in his way. He waved the subject aside with a rueful smile. 'We'd better say our cheerios to Donald. I'll be seeing him again soon – how did you find him?'

'I like him. Like him a lot. He's obviously got a sense of humour.'

'Oh yes, he has. Mind you, he has his off days, too.

Calls it the Black Dog, like Churchill. Can hardly blame him. Anyway, we must be going.'

We moved across to Donald, who was bidding farewell to the medical general and his lady. They exchanged pleasantries with us and then Donald, who was in high spirits, walked slowly with us to our cars, talking animatedly. He gave Mary and Sue a fond pat of a decorous sort, saw them installed in their respective seats and then turned back to me. His eyes rested on me appraisingly.

'I wish you a successful trip to the States. Always liked the place myself. I'm sorry we didn't get a chance for another chat about our friend Frewen. Too busy nattering, I'm afraid. Old man's problem.'

'Never mind,' I said. 'Another time, perhaps? If I can come back to you?'

'Of course. Delighted. Bore the pants off you on that subject. Any time; just give me a ring. As a matter of fact something did occur to me during the mêlée back there, while I was talking to someone else. It was your mention of his nickname: Mortal Ruin.' He grinned at the epithet.

'Oh really?'

'Yes. Jeremy may have told you I was a cavalryman once. It hit me after we'd spoken. Frewen had a younger brother called Stephen. Another hothead, he was. Got into a row with General French during the Boer War. Stephen Frewen was Colonel of the 16th Lancers by then; got mentioned in despatches for leading the charge at Klipdrift during the relief of Kimberley. Anyway, that's not my story. It was your gold shares that reminded me. During the late eighteen-eighties Frewen – Moreton, I mean – started playing the gold market madly on the London Stock Exchange. All the younger Frewen brothers had been left an inheritance, about sixteen grand each, which was a lot then. Anyway, Moreton persuaded Stephen to come in with him to give more power in the speculation. He tried to take on De Beers and the gold market single-handed. To cut a long story short, he lost the lot. The whole lot. Stephen's inheritance as well.'

A whicker from the stallion beyond the rails took his eyes away from me for a moment and, following his gaze, I saw the meadow again, with the fine September sunlight on it, the warm-tiled stables, the old house and the beautiful countryside. When I looked back, Donald's eyes were on me once more, less reflective, more intent as he spoke. 'It wasn't the City that gave Moreton that nickname, you know, Tim. It was the officers of the 16th Lancers, Stephen's friends. They called him Mortal Ruin.' His eyes went back to the stallion and I saw the affection in them as he spoke to me again, almost over his shoulder as he started going across to Jeremy's car. His voice was still humorous and animated, but there was an element of caution that wasn't entirely banter in the tone as he spoke. 'My advice to you, young man, if you're going to look at anything to do with Moreton Frewen and gold shares, is to keep a sharp eye out. A very sharp eye out. My father used to say that Frewen and gold were financial nitroglycerine. Pure high explosive. And my father, bless him, was never wrong about things like that.'

Chapter Four

The cheering thing about board meetings at Christerby's is that we normally retire to a private room at the Café Royal afterwards for lunch. This particular Friday's meeting was no exception. After a rather boring business session, with various motions and counter-motions which made the real world of hammer-banging numerous works of art seem remote, we had consumed a very tolerable meal and were sitting back with our coffees in a relaxed, mid-afternoon frame of mind. It was true that there were clouds on the business horizon; turnover had gone a bit static, margins were very pressed, American expansion was still tough going, but a nice easy profitable business with no aggravation doesn't exist nowadays, does it, what with internationl competition and governments shoving their oars in at every turn. We had given Howarth, the chief executive of the international company, a sympathetic hearing and I, for once, had not asked more than a handful of awkward questions.

Harry Howarth seemed to be going out of his way to be friendly to me. He was a solid, chunky man of about fifty, bald but not too fat, clad in a grey pinstripe suit, white shirt and neutral tie. He looked more like a successful industrialist than the head of a firm of fine art auctioneers, the sort of man you might see in Coventry or Birmingham or Manchester, dressed up for a day in London because his bank needed a bit of a talking-to. What remained of his hair was neat and short, only slightly speckled with grey around the ears, and his skin was a healthy tan, a light brown colour, as though he had been engaged in an energetic outdoor pastime rather than lying on a beach or under a sun lamp. I knew that he was well approved of by the banks and other institutions, had run successful international property investment businesses and had once been an advertising and PR consultant. He was a curious blend of smooth talker and brass-tacks realist, a man who owed his appointment to good contacts in both the City and the USA. I was placed to his left at the top of the lunch table, rather to my surprise, because he had seemed a bit suspicious at previous meetings. On his right was a man I hadn't met before: the new director of the American company, based in New York. This was Alexander Carlton, a classy name if you like, a man who had progressed to the board by working his way from the unusual background of being an art expert. I say unusual because a lot of art experts, as apart from art dealers, despite suspicious and inquiring minds, are not very businesslike or managerial. Carlton, however, seemed to possess these qualities, too. Sue had heard of him and told me his history, since he specialized, like her, in the Impressionists as well as American painting and Cubism. Well, I suppose Impressionism is *de rigueur* for anyone connected with auction art expertise these days, it being very much the top dog in the money stakes, so Carlton was well placed to understand the art market. He had studied in the States, London, Florence and Paris before doing a stint at the Metropolitan in New York, until someone – I think it may have been Howarth himself – lured him from the marble halls of Central Park to grubby commerce in the form of auctioneering. He was eminently suitable for Christerby's because he was Anglo-American, that splendid mix of blood, and sufficiently 'European' to be all things to all men in the art world of New York. His father was American, his mother English.

Next to him sat Charles Massenaux, Christerby's London expert on Impressionists and bronzes, now a director of the UK board. Charles is an old friend of mine despite being something of a smoothie; his dark brown hair flows in unobtrusive waves over his aristocratic head and his countenance is slightly saturnine, worldly, and immobile in that unimpressed cast that senior London auctioneers get. I really shouldn't make fun of Charles because I like him, and it was due to his intervention that White's picked up their substantial stake in the firm. Charles and I thus formed an axis, a relationship within the board that Howarth was doubtless aware of and which could not always have been too comfortable for him. Through Charles I had an inside line to the London end of operations and much house gossip on events in New York. Charles regarded my Art Fund with humorous disbelief and occasional admiration; like his competitors in the auctioneering world, he tended to speak condescendingly of it while rather wishing that he had got in on an art fund himself. Not that Charles isn't doing pretty well; from being head of department to getting a seat on the board when we helped to restructure it had done Charles a lot of good and had brought us a bit closer than our previous relationship, part-professional, part-friendly, had allowed.

'I thought you were very fair,' Howarth said at last, lighting a cigar and sitting back. 'I'm obliged to you for the copy, Tim.'

I made a self-deprecatory gesture. 'Thank you. It

seemed only right that you should have a copy of my report.'

He gave me a half-grin and a knowing look. 'I can guess that there's a bit of resistance to my plans for the States? That's why you've put things on record, so to speak?'

'Something like that. Well, not resistance exactly. Just, should we say, a need for clarification? A strategic rationale?'

His grin became broader. 'You're a tactful man, Tim. I can bet that Jeremy White is giving you problems. And if Jeremy's giving you problems, then White's board will be in a blind panic.'

I smiled. 'Jeremy has always been the most expansionist of the Whites. He's starting to pick up a few City traits these days, but his heart's still in the right place. He'll back you if he thinks there's half a chance of success.'

Howarth nodded slowly, but the new Alexander Carlton gave me a stare. 'You mean that the idea of the Chicago venture upsets the finance men that much?'

I nodded. 'They'd be happier about the idea if New York had turned the corner. A lot of money has gone into New York.'

'Surely it has turned the corner already? This year is going to be much better than last.'

'Oh yes, I know. But New York hasn't actually registered a profit yet, you see. Bankers always like to look at a black set of figures coming up, however temporarily, before you ask them for more money.'

Carlton pulled a face. 'Taking that philosophy to its logical conclusion, there'd be a hell of a lot of famous ventures in history that would never have attracted venture capital.'

'That's true. The problem is that history usually highlights the famous successes, the great achievements, rather than the hundreds more failures, the losses.' I thought for a moment of Moreton Frewen. 'Drake's treasure ship coming home loaded to the gunwales with Spanish silver is an image we all retain from school; we gloss over the sunk galleons, drowned seamen and ruined speculators because we prefer not to think about them. Bankers have a rather unflinching way of looking at balance sheets. We think of them as miserable pessimists, play-it-safe, non-risktakers. They say that if you want to gamble you can go to a casino.'

Carlton blinked. He was a thin man with gold spectacles, not much older than me, just a bit nearer forty, looking as though he had always lived his life indoors peering at impasto and X-ray photographs, but he was pleasant enough and shrewd in the way that art experts are; men used to tricks and deception and professional risk. He gave me a cautious smile. 'I thought you were a banker?' he queried. 'Are you saying that you don't associate yourself with your profession?'

Charles Massenaux permitted himself a broad smile as he leant in to the conversation. 'Now he's got you, Tim. You'll have to come off the fence and tell Alex just what you are.' He turned to Carlton, beside him. 'Tim's been running with the hares and chasing with the hounds for four years now.'

'I'm a *merchant* banker,' I said. 'That's a very broad-based calling, like the Church of England. It allows for a wide range of belief – and disbelief – to be accommodated within it.'

'Chicken! You're evading the question! You're not a merchant banker, either. I think you're still a management consultant *manqué*. You just like prying into other people's affairs and then telling them what to do.'

'How undignified. Quite wrong. I am a most respectable fellow these days. Prying into other people's businesses indeed. Me?'

Howarth laughed as he came back into the conversation. 'Yes, you. I have no doubt that you'll be prowling round this Chicago idea any day now, off on Concorde – '

'Concorde! We're not that extravagant, I'm afraid.'

'Well, off to the States anyway, just to snouse around.'

I gave him a disconcerted glance. 'As it happens, I am going to the States next week, but – '

'There you are!' Howarth blew an expensive and triumphant cloud of smoke upwards. 'I knew it! You'll be galloping over to see the Caseys, right there on the spot. Don't deny it!'

I shook my head. 'I will deny it. As it happens I am going to see Andy, but – '

'But! But! Come on, Tim, we've caught you out! Jeremy always works to pattern; I know him.'

I felt considerably defensive but Howarth was genial about this banter and I couldn't detect any malicious edge to it. He was still smiling broadly behind his cigar. From time to time he had winked at Charles and at Alex Carlton, who regarded me sceptically from behind his gold-rims.

'OK, we're bound to discuss it, but it's not the prime purpose of my visit. I have several things to catch up on with Andy Casey.'

'Oh really?' Carlton's voice had a tinge of irony in it. 'How convenient. Just at this time?'

'Yes. Just at this time.'

'What kind of things? Oh no – I'm *sure* they must be confidential?' He gave me a mocking look.

'Not all of them. Some are, some aren't. There are several joint ventures we have on at present.' I struggled to justify myself. 'There's even a thing concerning old gold-mine shares that a client needs advice on. That's not confidential; it should interest you lot, as auctioneers.'

'Old gold shares? Stocks, you mean? Stocks in old gold-mines? Or stocks in gold itself?' Carlton's interest perked up; his eyes had lost their mocking look.

'Mines. Gold-mines. An old client of Andy's has come by some old gold-mine shares. Utah and South Dakota. They belonged to an Englishman once, a man called Moreton Frewen, and – '

'Frewen?' Howarth put down his cigar. '*The* Moreton Frewen? The bimetallist? The one who lectured everyone?'

'Er, I'm not too sure about that, but yes, he was a bimetallist apparently. He had a bee in his bonnet about gold and silver.'

'How extraordinary. It must be the same man.'

I looked at Howarth curiously, seeing his broad, stocky figure stiffen from its relaxed pose as he leant forward to pick up his cigar again, tipping some ash off into a tray. 'Moreton Frewen,' he murmured. 'Gold shares? Him?'

'Well, they were his. Once. They or the envelope containing them have got his writing on them. He left them in the safekeeping of a sergeant for safety. At least that's what's written across them; keep with the sergeant for safety.'

'Extraordinary. They must go back a long way.'

'They do, I'm sure.' I looked across at Charles Massenaux. 'They may not be worth anything from the gold-mine point of view, but they might have value as documents. Like those old bonds people collect. What's it called? Something -ology?'

'Scrip-something-ology,' he said. 'Not quite our field, Tim. You need a specialist for that. Stanley Gibbons or someone.'

'Well, whatever. Andy asked me to find out anything I could about Frewen.' I looked at Howarth. 'Anything at all. Do I take it from your reaction that his name rings a bell?'

Howarth smiled. 'I do have a story about him.' He glanced at his watch and then at Carlton before turning to me. 'Alex is coming down to stay with us this weekend and I've promised my wife we'll be early. We have a cottage in the Cotswolds, you know, near Broadway. Gives me a chance for a bit of air after the week cooped up in London. I'll have to make it brief because we've just got time before the next train. Not that my story will help your gold-miner very much.'

'No?'

'I don't think so.' He pulled at the cigar. 'Part of my mother's family came from Canada. BC, actually. Vancouver and further north. Place called Prince Rupert. Ever heard of it?'

'Well, I've heard of it, of course, but not much else.'

'Ever been there?'

'No. No, I haven't.'

'You haven't missed much. Prince Rupert is a port at the end of the railway line. The old Grand Trunk route. Getting up towards Alaska. It was intended to be a new San Francisco. When it was decided that the line would end there a business entrepreneur called Hays, who was President of the Grand Trunk

Railway, decided to promote the place. He needed to attract investment to develop the town. He needed someone with good contacts, someone persuasive, someone who could tap the speculators among the wealthy upper crust of British and Canadian society. By pure chance he invited just the man he needed on a trip across Canada on his railroad, in his private coach.'

'Moreton Frewen?'

'Moreton Frewen. Hays persuaded Frewen to promote investment in Prince Rupert among his friends. The reward was an option on some of the best land for Frewen himself. He could take up the option if his efforts were successful and the price of land rose. Frewen was good at that sort of thing. He said it was a deal.'

'When was this?'

'Around 1906, I think. Frewen was down on his luck, back from Kenya which he also helped to promote. Anyway, he did his job only too well. They got all the investment they needed, Prince Rupert developed, and the price of land went up ten times.'

'Good old Frewen. So he made money that time?'

Howarth shook his head sadly. 'I'm afraid not. Hays and the Grand Trunk reneged on the deal. Frewen made the mistake of believing that Hays was a gentleman, like him, whose word was his bond. There was no written agreement even though the offer was made in front of witnesses. Hays got greedy. He wouldn't let Frewen have the option and he denied that the agreement existed. Frewen sued him and lost. Even the judge said that Frewen had been diddled, but they couldn't do anything about it legally.'

'What a bastard. Was there nothing Frewen could do?'

'Oh yes. That's where we come to the ironic bit. When Frewen's friends heard what had happened, they collared Hays. They were powerful men, who could make or break the Hays of this world. People like Lord Grey, who was Viceroy of Canada. They told Hays that if he didn't honour his agreement he was finished. Absolutely finished. They'd make sure he never did business in Britain or Canada again.' Howarth pulled on the cigar, which was burning down now, close to his lips. 'Hays knew that he was beaten. He capitulated. He agreed to let Frewen have his option, which was worth a fortune by then. This was agreed with Frewen's lawyer at the Savoy Hotel in London, just before Hays left to go back to Canada. They agreed to draw up the contract documents and send them on to him to be signed in Montreal. People like Hays and Frewen practically lived on the cross-Atlantic liners, you know; they were always buzzing to and fro.'

I restrained my impatience. 'So Frewen got his money?'

Howarth stood up, stubbing his cigar butt out. Fragrant smoke drifted away. He shook his head. 'Hays left for Canada immediately. He'd decided to cross on the very latest, the fastest, the best new steamship there was. Guess which one?'

'Oh no. Oh no!'

'Oh yes. It was 1912 by then. Hays sailed on the *Titanic*. No one ever saw him again.' He gestured to Carlton, who stood up to leave, and then looked down at me. 'That was the way with everything of Frewen's, Tim. Hays never signed the papers and Frewen never got the prime land, even though the case went on.

My advice to you, if you're going to get involved with anything to do with Moreton Frewen – anything at all – is to look out for yourself. Look out for yourself very carefully indeed.'

Chapter Five

'Jesus Christ.' A very large, white-haired police sergeant stood near me, looking about him with disbelief. 'You're trying to tell me that these men were mugging you?'

'Yes, they were.' I pushed myself off the barrier I was leaning on and stood upright. 'They grabbed my case and then went for me. Attacked me.'

A flicker went over his face. 'Are you British?'

'Yes, I am. I've just arrived.'

He stared at me impassively. Close to him, the young policeman had put his revolver away and was looking dubiously down at the dapper, grey-suited man, now no longer dapper, rocking to and fro and moaning as he held his leg. The lumber-jacketed one hadn't moved since collapsing but the concussed black man's eyelids were flickering in classic style. I didn't feel well; the side of my head ached horribly as feeling returned to it. I put my hand there.

'They hit you?' asked the sergeant curiously, as I made the movement.

'Yes.'

His eyes narrowed. 'What are you? What do you do?'

'I work for a bank. An investment bank.'

'A banker? You don't look like a banker to me.' He gestured at my cases, still flat on the ground beside the grey-suited man. 'What's in those cases that they were so anxious to get?'

'Nothing. Nothing special. Just my personal clothes. Business papers. Nothing valuable.'

'No? Well, we'll have to search them. Round here at O'Hare there's too many things come inside suitcases that people get excited about.' His eyes probed mine, making me start to get irritable.

'You can help yourself.' I took my hand off my head and looked right back at him. 'They're not locked. There's no gold bars or heroin or anything like that. Nothing. And the papers are just business papers, not the plans to the latest moon rocket. Or the President's love-letters.'

His expression didn't soften but I felt that I'd said something to reassure him somehow. He turned abruptly towards two of his men, still standing close by and staring at me. 'You call the medics?'

They nodded, without moving. 'On their way,' one of them said unemotionally, holding his truncheon down the seam of his trouser leg, as though pointing at a bug on the ground. The sound of aircraft, whistling jet engines and thunderous departures began to filter into my hearing. Nearby, I now saw people, ordinary civilians, grouped behind a policeman, staring at me. One pointed to the lumberjacketed man, who lifted a forearm from his sprawling, recumbent position and let it drop back again. Blood ran stickily from his nose and mouth. Unreality had taken over. This wasn't me, it wasn't happening to me, it was a dream, I was going to wake up, any minute from now, and Sue would nudge me and say hey, you were having a nightmare or something, you –

'Tim! For God's sake! Tim Simpson! What happened? What on earth is going on here?'

The big sergeant stiffened, swivelling his head. The

voice of Andy Casey bounced through the fogginess in my brain and I saw him striding towards me, a tall, lean, freckled man of my own age, as welcome a sight as I had ever seen anywhere. Andy Casey is about six foot three, and stringy in build, but he looks fit and alert, grey-suited and sober, like a model for any respectable citizen. His face was incredulous.

'Tim? I'm sorry, I got delayed and – what the heck? What on earth has been going on here? Who are these guys all over the ground?'

'I'm afraid there's been a spot of bother, Andy. I'm very, very glad to see you.'

He gaped at me. The big sergeant gave a jerk of his head in my direction. 'You know this man? You here to meet him?'

'Yes, of course, I – ' Andy gave a sudden infectious grin. 'You mean there's been a fight here? Already? Heck, I was only ten minutes late, we had a break-in, I got delayed. I expected to find you over in the main arrival hall. What – what happened? Will someone tell me?'

'They tried to pinch my case. My cases. When I ran after them and argued they attacked me.'

'Three of them? Three of them attacked you? And you laid 'em all out cold like this?'

'No, no. Not three of them. Two of them – those two – they attacked me and that third one ran off with my cases. At least, he tried to. I kicked his leg.'

'He looks like he's crippled for life.'

'I wish he were.' I began to feel sour. 'But he'll get better. In rather a long time.'

Andy gave a snort of emotion of some kind and turned to the sergeant. 'I can vouch for Mr Simpson here. My name is Casey. I'm with Owens, McLeod and Casey, downtown. Here, I have a card. And plenty of ID.' He handed over a card to the big, black-uniformed man so that the policeman could read the legend I knew well. 'Andrew O'Brien Casey,' it would say, 'Vice-President, Owens, McLeod and Casey. Investment Bankers.' The sergeant stared down at it, a tiny white rectangle in his huge red hand. It struck me then, looking at his features and his white hair, that this sergeant was Irish, well, not really Irish, but American Irish, like Andy. His build was huge, like some of the Hibernian rugby players I've been up against, and played with, and his name was probably Daley or Houlihan or Mulvagh or Donahue or something like that.

'Maguire,' he said, interrupting my thoughts and looking up from the little white card. 'I'm Maguire. Say, haven't I met you somewhere? Aren't you the Casey that's on the funding committee at St Peter's? Andy Casey? The banker?'

'Why – why, yes.' Andy looked at the sergeant with an affirmative but puzzled expression. That was a surprise; Andy is, I know, a practising Catholic, but he'd never mentioned any charitable activities to me.

The sergeant stuck out his fist. 'Tom Maguire. We met at the reception for the chapel restoration – the opening last April?'

Andy grabbed his hand. 'Of course! Tom Maguire! I'm sorry – I didn't recognize you with the, er, the –'

'Uniform?' The big sergeant chuckled. 'I guess not. It does disguise a man, now, doesn't it? And this, um, this British gentleman has come here to do business with you? You know him?'

'Yes. Absolutely. As I said, I can vouch for him. Tim Simpson is a friend and a banker too. Those muggers jumped the wrong man.'

'They certainly did. Wait here a moment, please.'

With a wry smile, Maguire wheeled on the two policemen standing nearby and altered his tone. 'Well, come on! Let's move it here! Get that ambulance through. And keep those people moving! It's all over, folks. All over.' He beckoned to the young policeman whose revolver had given me such a fright. 'Go with those three and make sure they're booked. Don't let them out. OK?'

'OK, Sergeant.' The young one gave a brisk nod and then, hesitating, gestured at the grey-suited bag-snatcher, still writhing on the ground. 'We've pulled him in before, haven't we? Isn't he called Kamrowski, or something like that?'

'I know who he is,' Maguire growled. 'I've seen him before, too. And he's Kamrowski. Book him and keep him for me.' He began to issue more instructions and moved away from us as the tableau of watching people was stirred into movement and my damaged attackers were shepherded or loaded into suitable vehicles. Suddenly it seemed as though the whole episode was over; the airport was returning to normal again. I saw an aircraft lift away into the distance, smelt aviation fuel, felt cold air on my face.

Andy touched my arm. 'Are you OK, Tim? You look very pale.'

'I'll be all right in a minute. The air's clearing my head.'

'I'm really sorry I was late. We had a break-in this morning. Or rather last night. They called me from a meeting on the other side of town to check my office to see if anything was missing. That held me up.'

'Oh dear. Was it serious?'

'Nope. Nothing. Well, a bit of petty cash. All the real securities are kept safe. These small-time crooks see the plate saying "bankers" on the door and think the place is full of money. There was nothing much for them to take. Made a hell of a mess, though.'

'What – in your office?'

'You bet. And some of the others. Turned everything over. Papers everywhere. Ah, here comes the sergeant – Tom Maguire. I knew he was a policeman, but I've never seen him in uniform before. I only met him once. St Peter's is on West Madison, right around the corner from the office. It's kind of our local church, not for home and Sundays, you understand, but right near us downtown.'

The large white-haired sergeant stood in front of me and peered carefully into my face, searching my eyes with his own. 'Are you OK? Do you want to go for medical treatment? Maybe you should.'

'No, thanks. I'm all right, really I am. I took just the one big thump.'

'Sure? Sorry if I was a bit suspicious back there. We'll still have to check your cases, like I said, just for the record.'

'No problem.'

'Good. Thank you.' He smiled at me for the first time. 'I hope you'll excuse my asking, but were you perhaps a boxer or something, once?'

Andy grinned. 'No, Tom, he's not a boxer, despite his appearance. Tim here was once a rugby football player, a very distinguished one, over in England. He played for Cambridge University.'

Maguire nodded his black-hatted head sagely. 'Now I understand. Those three guys certainly did pick the wrong man.' He held out his huge fist. 'Pleased to make your acquaintance. Sorry if there was a misunderstanding.'

I shook with him. 'Not at all. No offence taken.'

'Fine. Good. Well, I'll have to ask you to come

with me to clear up all the formalities. If Mr Casey here doesn't mind following us, he can take you on afterwards. We'll try to make it as quick as possible.' He walked over to a patrol car and held the door open. 'After all, if you've come over to see Mr Casey on business, you won't want to hang around here, will you?'

Chapter Six

The offices of Owens, McLeod and Casey are in the La Salle Bank Building, spang in the centre of Chicago's Loop business district. It's an older sort of skyscraper but still pretty tall, entered on the ground floor via a long, pinkish-marbled arcade of shops with lifts in the middle. If you could lean out of the correct back window, you might look out over the square in front of the main Post Office nearby on Dearborn and Adams, which has a modern red iron sculpture by Calder in it, resembling a sagging anchor but actually entitled Flamingo. Up in the company's conference room, however, tens of floors above ground, one is not tempted into doing much leaning out, even though, from time to time, I speculated on whether, if I did so and for far enough, I would be able to see right to the top of Michigan Avenue where it meets the Chicago River, and squint at the site of Fort Dearborn, marked in brass plates across the street to show where Captain John Whistler the Anglo-Ulsterman put up the palisades one hundred and eighty-odd years ago.

Over the prime fireplace position in the panelled conference room, the painting by his grandson James of that celebrated artist's English mistress, Maud Franklin, looked down at me with a pinched but knowing expression. It was a full-length portrait of her, hand on hip, carrying a muff. During our meetings, Andy Casey had seen me glance at it and had smiled an understanding smile as he silently recalled, like me, the way in which it had got there. Neither of us mentioned it, but he knew it gave me pleasure to see it and, like our own painting of Wapping, I admired it as a work of art. Even those purists down at the Tate Gallery will admit that Whistler painted some smashing pictures.

I was feeling a lot better. My head didn't ache any more. I had had two very good nights' sleep at the Palmer House Hotel, not far away. My brain felt clear; and assurance from the police sergeant, Tom Maguire, that the attack at the airport was nothing personal or premeditated helped to release my thoughts for business and prevent any morbid worry about any deeper implications. Maguire was very reassuring on the point.

'A bunch of small-time pros,' he told us on the telephone during the second day. 'They work the stations and the airports. I guess they took you for a sucker when you put down your case in the foyer. The only real craftsman is Kamrowski – the grey guy who actually lifted the case. He's been around a while and has a record; usually he's too clever to catch. The other two strike me as being pretty dumb. No ulterior motive as far as we can tell or that they will admit. Just a random hit on a new arrival.'

With this unemotional, calming report, I felt free to work unencumbered by larger suspicions. In a life which has had its fair share of sinister, carefully-timed aggression, there is a tendency to think of every such happening as being the work of some Master Planner, intent on mangling Simpson as part of a grand strategy too complex to comprehend. This time I was cheerfully able to ascribe the attack to part of Chicago's impersonal crime statistics, like those of any major city anywhere. Soon, Andy and I were enmeshed in the doings of our competitors in the Chicago area, the implications of opening up a new auction house in a major city, and a welter of statistics and crystal-ball gazing. We could leave my attackers safely to Maguire; it was useful to have Andy Casey's solid reputation and church contacts to establish my well-being in Chicago. Charity may begin at home, I thought, but in Andy's case it certainly has spread itself out to finish elsewhere. Without Andy, Maguire might have been much more difficult.

Andy, however, had his mind on other things. He was quite excited, for a Chicagoan. 'That guy Frewen I asked you about was amazing! Quite amazing! I mean, Tim, I'm grateful to you for those stories you told me, but this is a city built on cattle, originally, and Frewen was a cattle man, back in Wyoming. Do you know what that crazy Englishman tried to do?'

'No.'

'He tried to take on the Chicago Beef Trust!'

'The what?'

'The Chicago Beef Trust. Back in the 1880s. Can you imagine? The big boys. Armour, Swift, Morris and McNeil. I mean, we here at OMC started life as hide shippers, so it wasn't difficult to get the story from some of the old records here in the city. Those guys – the Beef Trust – dominated the stockyards. Frewen understood distribution only too well. His herds were on the Powder River in Wyoming. He had to drive them five hundred miles to the Missouri at Omaha, then load 'em on rail to Chicago. The stockyards bought the herds, fattened them up and sold them for meat. They made the big money. A lot of the meat went to England, either already killed or on the hoof for slaughter when it got to Liverpool or somewhere like that. What Frewen did was to try and cut out the middleman. He even tried to get the law changed in England so that he could import cattle and fatten them on farms over there, instead of having them slaughtered at the port of entry.' Andy shook his head in wonder at the thought of the scale of such a thing; the idea of changing the whole basis of the cattle industry. 'When they wouldn't change the law in England – lucky for Chicago that they didn't – he decided to cut out Chicago anyway. He bought land near Duluth, right at the western point of Lake Superior. A thousand acres. He built cattle sheds and fattened the cattle on free grain, rejected from the screenings at the wheat silos. The Beef Trust cut the price of dressed beef by half to try and ruin him. He fought back and he might even have won. Apparently, Frewen was the leader of the Wyoming Stock Growers Association in Cheyenne; he had the ear of the President of the USA and the Viceroy of Canada. The trouble was that the ranges were getting overstocked. There were too many cattle and too many settlers and rustlers moving in to steal steers and mavericks. Then they had two dreadful winters: 'eighty-four and 'eighty-five. Frewen knew by 1884 that the end was in sight. He cabled his directors in England to sell out before the collapse.'

'Don't tell me,' I interrupted him. 'I can guess what happened, so you don't have to be polite. They behaved like classic British boards of directors back in England and did nothing.'

'I'm afraid you've got it. They didn't follow his advice. Frewen's own contract didn't allow him to sell out his share. They all lost their shirts. And pants. Frewen landed up heavily in debt. The land near Duluth became West Superior City and there are streets with his name there, but Frewen had to sell all that. Six years later, the land was worth ten times what he sold it for.'

'Good grief.'

'It was a hell of a crash. A lot of English and Scottish investors lost on cattle at that time. About ten million sterling, they reckon. Frewen was just another casualty statistic. He closed down the Powder River Ranch – it had a huge log cabin called Castle Frewen – and went back to England.'

'Disastrous. I'd no idea he was such a baron.'

'Oh, sure he was. He was quite a legend, Tim. I mean, when he and his brother Richard first went to Wyoming it was real frontier country. The Sioux were still dangerous – the Big Horn battle was still fresh in everyone's minds. Frewen knew Bill Cody well, and all the local bigwigs. When he led the Stock Growers he had a house in Cheyenne with leather on the walls. It's still called Sir Moreton Frewen's house. He entertained visiting British aristocracy at the Powder River with champagne and all the trimmings. Everything was in great style. Brought his wife out from New York in the Deadwood stage. He was a cattle baron, damn it. They lynched rustlers in those days and he knew it. Ever read Owen Wister's book called *The Virginian*?'

'No, I haven't.'

'Well, one of the local rustler-hangings figures in that. I've never seen that film rubbish called *Heaven's Gate*, but in 1892 Frewen was in Washington during the Johnson County War. He was busted from ranching by then, but he got Senator Blaine to send troops from Fort McKinney to relieve the besieged cattle owners, some of whom were his friends. Otherwise the rustlers would have hanged them. That was his account, anyway. He was a hell of a high talker, Tim.

No one knew quite whether to believe him or not. He could ride and he could hunt and he was tough, that's for sure. A tall guy with a moustache and sharp blue eyes. In those days a cattle boss always carried a gun and Frewen was no exception.'

Andy paused, slightly out of breath. I hadn't seen him that excited for months. History is not usually your average American's favourite subject but this bit of it had grabbed Andy, all right. It was as though the smell of the stockyards, dust, leather, the far high ranges of Wyoming and the great revolver-toting story of the Wild West had suddenly come to life for him. I tried to steer the conversation back to the original point.

'What about the gold?'

'Gold? Gold? Hell, you can't separate Frewen from gold! He was always after gold! Mines, processes – he financed a patent crusher made by a Scotsman called Crawford – everything. When he came out to Wyoming, in 1878, the rush was on in the Black Hills.' He grinned happily. 'It was like a stampede, Tim. South Dakota borders on Wyoming. Wild, lawless things happened. Deadwood is right there in the Black Hills, and the famous stagecoach got held up regularly. They killed all the passengers a couple of times and left the bodies right there for the varmints to find. Just like the Indians did here at Fort Dearborn.'

'This was the same stagecoach? The one Frewen brought his wife out in?'

'The same damn one. She was Clara Jerome, Tim. Her sister was your Winston Churchill's mother. The Jeromes were big time in New York. Hell, Leonard Jerome, he – '

'Wait! Andy, wait! You're going too fast for me. I

have to go on to New York after this. Am I going to get a chance to see these famous shares, stocks, whatever?'

'Oh, gee, Tim, I'm sorry. Of course you are.' He chuckled and shook his head at himself. 'I wouldn't be telling you all this otherwise. The guy who has them is an old client of ours called Victor Perkins. Been in real estate and other business all his life. He came by these stocks as part of a complex swap I won't bore you with. We haven't got them here because he doesn't think they're that valuable and he has a safe in his house out near Sunset Valley golf course. I haven't seen them yet but I'm going out there tomorrow to look at the documents. D'you want to come? I figured you would.'

'I'd love to.'

'Great. Victor'll be pleased to meet someone from England. His family was from Wales, way back. It seems that these stocks were kept by someone who moved to Chicago in the 'twenties. Mines in Utah and Colorado and South Dakota. The only mine still going in South Dakota, as far as I know, is the Homestake, and none of these stocks are in that. But they're in a big old envelope addressed to Mr Moreton Frewen of Brede Place, Sussex – you were right about that, or at least Jeremy was. Bang on, what he said about the Frewens being an old Sussex family. This Moreton must have been quite an adventurer. I had no idea until we did our researches that he was Winston Churchill's uncle. Victor Perkins will be delighted. He'll love it. It's a bit of history for him. They might have some value as documents, even if the gold-mines turn out to be a busted flush.'

'Can you check that?'

'Oh, sure we can. If he wants us to. It would take

time, mind, so it would cost money. Perkins might want to do that himself, since he's retired and got plenty of time. But of course I figured to include you on my next visit to him, before you head over to New York.' He grinned. 'Knowing your propensity for history, I – '

The phone rang, interrupting him, and he scowled at it as he made an irritated noise.

'I told them not to disturb us.'

The phone rang again, insistently. Andy got up from the table, strode across to the side of the room and picked up the instrument.

'This is Casey. I left a message I didn't want – hey? Who? Oh. Oh, OK, put him on.'

He clasped a hand over the receiver. 'It's Perkins's son, Frank. Sorry. I guess I have to take this one. Seems like it's important.' He took his hand off the mouthpiece. 'Hello? This is Andy Casey here. Hi. Hi, Frank. How are you? I – '

Silence overtook him. He stood awkwardly, the phone to his ear, half turning to me, half to the wall at the side of the room. All the time the phone was pressed to his ear, the unheard voice talking on and on, his eyes were on mine. Not so much to start with, but more and more as the call continued, so that his stare intensified, narrowed, focused. It was a stare I'd seen in other people before, an unbelieving yet comprehending stare, accusatory almost, as though everything he was hearing, the shock, the disbelief yet the swiftly-following belief, the horror, the numb awareness of loss, could be engendered by my presence or attributed in some way to my involvement. When he put the phone down his face was white.

'Victor Perkins has been murdered,' he said.

'What?'

'Murdered. There was a break-in last night. Burglars. They made him open the safe. They took everything and they killed him. Shot him.' His voice was not normal, not in key or in steadiness. 'They shot Victor. There was hardly anything worth killing anyone for in that safe.' His eyes came back to mine. 'But they took everything. Including those gold-mine stocks. All of them. There's absolutely nothing left. The envelope I told you about, Moreton Frewen's envelope, went with everything else.' His stare was burning into me now, his eyes white, his face drained. 'What the hell could anyone have wanted that envelope for?'

Chapter Seven

I stayed at the St Regis in New York. It's on Fifth Avenue, fairly high up to the right if you're looking at a map of mid-Manhattan, and therefore quite accessible to the big auctioneers, but not too far from what I still think of as the centre of events. The big auctioneers, in case you didn't know, are further up and well over to the right, over to the east in places like York Avenue, where their overheads are not as high as their first, mistaken addresses. It makes them still convenient for the high-spending elite of upper Madison Avenue and all that crowd. Christerby's New York premises are up that way and, after I had checked in to the hotel, I headed in that direction. Life has to go on, despite its calamities, and I had left Andy Casey in Chicago after what I hoped was a suitably decent interval. He was very, very upset. I knew what was on his mind; my violent arrival, his break-in, and then Perkins's death. It was as though the fact of my involvement had dictated such events, but he didn't want to say that. Andy is a decent, responsible citizen, and if he thought that Perkins's murder could be traced back to our inquiries, in no matter how remote a way, he would take it very badly. I tried to reassure him with Maguire's comforting report. I also suggested that his break-in was quite unconnected. I could tell that he wanted to believe me, but that doubts nagged him. I left him making preparations to go to Perkins's funeral and tried to drop the whole thing from my mind. It doesn't do to dwell on these things at length; the mind constructs all sorts of horrid scenarios when prompted to wander its way down the avenues of imagination in circumstances like those.

Big auctioneers are addicted to impressive foyers in their buildings so that clients can throng there. Ours was no exception. I say ours because, despite my principal allegiance to the Bank, I am a director of Christerby's and have a certain feeling of belonging, which made the deference I was greeted with by the foyer receptionist all the more enjoyable.

'Mr Simpson, sir? Welcome back to New York. It's nice to see you again. How are you?'

'Well, thank you.' That marked me as a foreigner, for a start. An American would have said good, thank you, with that strange love of ungrammatical usage that they have.

'Fine. Mr Carlton is expecting you. Please go right up.'

Alexander Carlton's office is above the foyer, on the first floor. You can take the lift or, like me, stride up a fairly wide staircase, with beige marble treads, to a carpeted landing. His secretary, in an ante-room, was already standing up and moving to greet me by shaking hands in a way that few English secretaries ever would. She was very attractive, so that an excuse to clasp her hand was all the more welcome. She smiled at me quite fondly, I thought.

'Hi! Mr Simpson. How are you?'

'I'm well, thank you. How are you?'

'Good, thank you, good. Alexander is expecting you. Would you like some coffee?'

'Love some.'

'Fine. I'll bring it right in after you.'

There's something about a warm welcome from an

attractive woman that puts the Simpson constitution into a eupeptic state, so I tripped lightly through the next office door on lilting feet only to get a mild shock.

' 'Morning, Tim.' Harry Howarth's matter-of-fact, brass-tacks voice had an amused ring to it as he stood up from a chair in front of Alexander Carlton's desk. He swung round to greet me and grinned, a sturdy, grey-blocked figure which contrasted with the thinner, ascetic look of Carlton, who had also risen to come round his desk and greet me. 'Didn't expect to see me here, did you? I told Alex we'd give you a start when you got here. Now you see me, now you don't, hey?'

I recovered my poise and shook hands with his firm grasp. 'What a surprise. A pleasant surprise, I must say. Hello, Harry. Hello, Alex. How are you both? This is an unexpected pleasure.'

Howarth chuckled. 'I came over two days ago. Not by Concorde, if you're thinking what you bankers normally think. I don't believe in lashing out too much money on air fares. Business class is quite good enough for me. But things are moving here and we need to get on, so I came over. Ah, here comes coffee. You're looking well, Tim, and – good grief! What on earth have you done to your face? You've not been back on the rugger field, have you?'

I put a hand to the right side of my jaw, which, as I had turned to shake hands, must have come into stronger light. It wasn't really painful any more, nor was it swollen now, but I knew that there was still a fading, bluish-yellow mark, quite large, on the lower side, against the bone. Carlton, Howarth and the secretary all clustered round me and stared at it in embarrassing concern.

'What happened to you?'

'Do you need any treatment? Can I get you something?'

The secretary was proving to be more and more attractive. 'We have medication in the furniture hall where the porters sometimes – '

'No, no.' I waved my hands about. 'You're very kind. Thank you, it's perfectly OK. It's all over now. I had a brush with some muggers.'

'Muggers?' they chorused in horror, as though the States almost never, indeed very rarely, experienced such dreadful things. 'Were you badly hurt? Did they steal everything?'

'No.' I gestured at my briefcase. 'They tried to take my luggage. At Chicago airport. But they didn't get anything. It's all intact.'

'But you had to let them take something? Wallet? Watch?'

'Er, no. No, I didn't.'

'You mean – ' the secretary's voice went into a thrilled, awestruck tone – 'you resisted them? You fought them?'

'Um, yes. I'm afraid I'm a bit possessive about my kit. Unwise, perhaps. But I did.'

'But what happened? How many were there?' She was wide-eyed now; very flattering it was.

'Three. I had a bit of luck, actually. A chance right hook hit the bullseye and laid one out. Only one of the other two was up to much and I managed to do for him. Touch and go, but I was lucky.'

'But weren't they armed?' Her mouth was open.

'No. Not really. Well, a knife. Managed to avoid that.'

'And you – you *dealt with* all three of them.'

'Er, yes. More or less. The police arrived eventually.'

Howarth suddenly burst into a roar of laughter and clapped me on the back, gripping my shoulder in what seemed like affection. 'Fantastic! Tim, you mad dog! I might have guessed! Of all the men a mugger should leave alone, Simpson must be number one. What a useful citizen! Not a document lost! Eh, Alex? What did I tell you? He was one of the most aggressive forwards the game ever saw. That's our boy! Eh?'

Carlton smiled rather thinly and took off his gold-rimmed spectacles. 'Extraordinary. I must say it is unusual. To be honest, Tim, it was very foolhardy to do that. Resist, I mean. It is very dangerous. Most of these muggers are very, very violent. They'll kill you. Without a thought. The standard advice to everyone is to give them just what they want. If you hold things up, delay them I mean, they get psychotic. Really awful. Please don't do anything like that if it happens here in New York, please. They have guns. They'll shoot you dead, for sure.'

'Ah. Er, yes. I'm sure you're right. But still, it won't happen here, will it? I mean, I'll stick to a safe tack here.'

'Good. I'd feel terrible if I hadn't warned you.' Carlton replaced his glasses and smiled with more warmth. 'We need you on our side, Tim. Hate to have anything happen to you while you're here. Let's have that coffee.'

The secretary was still looking at me with pure adulation. I'd forgotten that America, a violent place, still tends to over-admire the man who can defend himself with aggression. She was a brunette, about thirty, with a mature ripeness that made me suddenly conscious that I'd been away from Sue for several days and had been working hard, concentrating on facts and figures, quite apart from the other incidents in Chicago. I pulled myself together and managed not to leer at her too lustfully as she took the coffee from Howarth and insisted on serving me herself. We sat down round a low table in one corner of the office and the secretary left, swaying out to give a rear view that brought an even stronger pang of desire before the door closed.

'So how's it going?' Howarth was nothing if not straight to the point. 'Is it thumbs up or down for Chicago?'

I smiled carefully. 'I haven't got all the facts yet. Andy Casey and I have gone through a great deal of material and considerable analysis. I need information from you, now.'

'Really?' Howarth glanced at Carlton. 'What sort of information?'

I explained to them carefully how the assessment we were doing was calculated, and what sort of information had to be built into our model before we could run final analyses. What I particularly wanted was the source of current business by geographical area, if that was possible, and an assessment from each of their specialists on how much business in each category was volatile in the geographical sense. Would the business move or not if offered a Chicago facility, how much was prestige, New York-only business; things like that. Howarth rubbed his hands together vigorously when I finished.

'This is excellent! Excellent! Alex, can you dig out the info that Tim needs?'

'I should think so.' Carlton was cautious, reserved, keeping to his precise persona, the one that seemed more like a cost-and-works accountant than an auctioneer and art expert. 'It may take a little time to dig out, of course, but we'll do our best. And you're welcome to talk to our specialists. How long will you need?'

I put my coffee down carefully. 'Er, hang on a moment. This idea of opening in Chicago is your idea, Christerby's idea, I mean. You must surely have done some assessments yourselves? You must have some facts and estimates prepared already? I mean, my work is for White's, really. As a sort of back-up.'

Carlton gave one of his thin, wry smiles and looked deliberately at Howarth, who had started to grin like a Cheshire cat. 'I can't say that we have, Tim.' He let his voice go humorous. 'It's our idea of course, and we're serious about it. But there's no point in keeping a dog and barking yourself, is there? Sorry for the analogy, but I said to Alex that as soon as we moot the idea and Tim reports it to Jeremy White, we'll have White's best man clambering all over the place to check the idea. So why use up our own valuable resources? There's no one in Christerby's who'll do a better objective assessment than one of their experts, never mind what our gut feeling is. We'll get a professional analysis to check it out. And so it was; we got White's best man: Tim Simpson.' He grinned at me wolfishly. 'More coffee?'

'You – you fiend. You cunning, devious, good-for-nothing, property-dealing, advertising, PR-flannelling so-and-so!'

'Ha, ha!' He was laughing genuinely, with pure pleasure. 'You flatter me! I'm glad I've got your admiration. Words like that from Tim Simpson are gold, Alex, pure gold – which reminds me: how did the Frewen thing go? Another Klondike?' He poured out coffee with zestful enjoyment.

I shook my head sadly. 'I'm afraid not. Things didn't turn out so well.'

'Why not?'

I told them what had happened, not bothering with a long account of Frewen's cattle dealings, but giving a short version of old Victor Perkins's fate. It seemed to affect them almost as much as it did me. Telling someone else about it for the first time like that made me realize just how the murder had upset my visit to Chicago. I hadn't known Perkins, but I felt a dreadful sense of loss; I'd been looking forward to seeing him, quite apart from the thrill of holding those shares and their envelope, the historical link.

'How bloody awful,' Howarth said. 'Ghastly. Jesus! You have had a bad time, Tim. My dear chap. You must be upset. How did Andy Casey take it?'

'Very badly, I'm afraid. He somehow felt responsible.'

'Oh no. It can't have been any fault of his. But how dreadful. Appalling. That sort of thing makes you feel sick.'

'It does.' Carlton showed, if anything, even more concern. 'I'm afraid that life in big cities is becoming increasingly dangerous. The violence is horrifying. I hate it.' He shook his head sadly. 'And the documents are completely lost?'

'Yes. All gone. There's no sign of them.'

'How futile. Were they valuable?'

'We're not sure. Andy's trying to find out. He's going to phone me.'

'What a pity. I was quite looking forward to hearing all about them. Harry got me quite interested in this man Frewen. After all, we are in what was once his father-in-law's city. But that interest of mine pales before a tragedy of this sort.'

'I don't understand, sorry. His father-in-law?'

'Leonard Jerome. Didn't you know? He was King of Wall Street for a long spell. A fantastic man. Had a huge house on Madison Square with a private opera house attached to it. He was one of those larger-than-life characters.' Carlton smiled meaningfully. 'Jerome was keen on opera and its singers. Jenny Lind – he named his daughter after her – Patti, Fanny Ronalds, all those. He was a great yachtsman, too. Up at Newport, Rhode Island. Backed those cross-Atlantic races between British and American yachts before the America's Cup existed. That's how the family came to be at Cowes in the Isle of Wight. If Jerome hadn't been keen on yachting, Lord Randolph wouldn't have met Jennie. And then there would have been no Winston. Americans love that kind of story, Tim.'

'We're not unattracted to that kind of story ourselves. So Moreton Frewen must have been here a lot?'

'You bet. He knew all Jerome's contacts – Lorillard, Belmont, the Roosveldts – not that he didn't meet them in England, too. Frewen must have been well in with the top four hundred. Jerome lost a lot of money in his later years, but he was devoted to his daughters. He died in England, you know. Brighton.'

I spilled coffee into my saucer and on to the table as I gave an involuntary jerk. They sprang to mop up.

'What's the matter? Are you all right?'

'Sorry. Stupid of me. Just a bad reflex. It's nothing.' I tried to hide my fluster. 'Caught my arm the wrong way.'

To those of you who don't know, Brighton has

figured only too prominently in a number of unpleasant episodes in my past. Mention of the place is enough to cause the Simpson reflexes to jerk spasmodically. If any investigation, project, or art purchase features Brighton on its itinerary, I bridle like a horse confronted by a whistling loco. The very remote fact that Leonard Jerome died in Brighton was enough to give me severe palpitations about the whole Frewen-Jerome involvement. It was with relief that I found that the interruption had turned their minds back to the Chicago auction venture again and we started to work out a programme with names, timing and soothing professional routine. At the end of our meeting Howarth took me out for a very respectable lunch; Carlton excused himself on the grounds of work but, in fact, New Yorkers these days don't go in for business lunches much, nor for midday drinking, so I guessed that his rather spare frame eschewed such luxuries as a matter of principle. Howarth, however, was in robust form and did his food full justice.

'I hope you don't feel too aggrieved about my little subterfuge,' he said almost apologetically over coffee. 'Quite honestly, Tim, Christerby's haven't got the resources to do a proper assessment and I'd have had to call in consultants. Doing it this way we got something much better.'

'Flatterer.'

He smiled. 'Alex is a good man for our purposes but he's a bit light on that sort of business experience. What do you think of him?'

'He seems OK.' Caution lights flashed in my brain; I wasn't sure what Howarth was fishing for. 'He's an art expert, which helps, and he's very international. He can attract business and he understands the working of the markets. The accountants can support him from an internal, cost-catching point of view. He's a bit cold, perhaps. Why?'

'Oh, nothing. Just value your judgment. I agree with you on the whole. I think he can run New York for us, providing we back him up well. Which means provided I back him up well. Fortunately, thanks to Charles, London is looking after itself pretty well. What I'm not sure of is whether Alex can look after a country-wide organization here in the States. That might need a different animal.'

'Ah, I see. I'm not sure about that. I'd have to know him a bit more. People very often grow into jobs like that, Harry.'

'That's a consultant's answer.' He grinned. 'A merchant banker would shoot from the shoulder and say yes or no.'

I scowled at him. 'Merchant banking isn't about the pheasant-shooting landed gentry any more. It's a modern business.'

He banged the table. 'Well answered! Actually, I agree. I'll talk to you about it again sometime, if I may. We have to get on, right now.'

He stood up and I got a full view of him, stocky, stalwart, all-of-a-piece, with his Lancashire name and his Lancashire manner that seemed odd in an ex-property and advertising man running a fine art auctioneers, but which fitted the role very well. It occurred to me that he and Jeremy would probably get on together splendidly if they didn't clash too much in these early days. They were both forthright, uncomplicated in their strange ways, so that you knew where you were with them. We parted genially.

It was a warm autumn in New York. The buildings there seem to stoke up heat during the summer and retain it, which makes the later part of the year much warmer than you get in London. I spent the next two days in and out of Christerby's New York rooms, working fairly hard. A couple of phone calls had me checking that Sue was all right; she was. It was one evening that the call I had rather been dreading came through, while I was working in my room at the hotel, with papers strewn all around me.

'Tim? Hi. Andy Casey.' His voice wasn't taut but it wasn't relaxed either.

'Hello, Andy. What news?'

'We've got nothing on the burglary. Not yet. I've asked Tom Maguire if he'll keep an eye out for me.' There was a silence. 'One of the advantages of having connections is that you can sometimes get an inside line on things.'

'Of course. What about the Frewen gold connection?'

There was a sigh. 'Jesus, Tim. You wouldn't believe the difficulties. Frewen was all over. I've had one of our researchers working full time. I feel I owe it to Perkins. My people have even been to the Frewen papers at the Library of Congress.'

'The what?'

'The Moreton Frewen papers in the Library of Congress. Didn't you know? That guy got into everything. He knew every President personally from Hayes to Wilson. But never mind that; I've traced his involvement in the Eureka – that's the Centennial Eureka at Cane Springs, Utah – then the Lewiston at Colorado Springs, and then there was Cripple Creek and, later, the Oroville Dredging –'

'Hey! Hang on! Hang on, Andy. Slow down. Were these the ones that Perkins had?'

'No – well, I'm not sure – but we may have some

luck there. Frank Perkins, the son, says that his father sent the list of shares to a specialist to see whether any of the mines is still in production or worth anything. We're going to trace them that way. But I've been getting all this research done because I want to satisfy myself on all this. I need to check out all this Frewen gold involvement. I want to know about it. Really know.'

'Andy,' I said, as gently as I could, 'isn't this going a bit far? Shouldn't you wait until the police do their work? What does Tom Maguire say?'

'Oh, he says that all these different events are pure coincidence.' Andy's voice was impatient. 'That's hogwash, Tim. I know it is. Damn it, I know there's more to this than just coincidence. I know it! Someone rifled my office, tried to get your papers, killed old Perkins. It can't all just be coincidence. There's a connecting link.' His voice rose. 'My belief is that Frewen has something to do with it.'

'Hey, Andy! Take it easy. This is me, Tim, remember? You're starting to sound obsessive. Aren't you reading a bit too much into it all?'

There was a moment's hesitation. 'I – I don't think so. I know Tom Maguire doesn't agree with me. But what about you? You must have had the same thought, Tim, with your experience? Haven't you thought about it? What do you think?'

His voice was sharp. He was coming out with it at last, it was taking an emotional effort, but he was putting into words the things I knew he had avoided saying to my face in Chicago. Of course I'd thought through the same things. I shook my head as I thought of Leonard Jerome and Brighton, such an ominous pointer, and shivered a superstitious shiver.

'I've thought about it, Andy, but I can't possibly

explain it. Life can't be like that. How did anyone know I was coming, for instance?'

'They broke into my office the night before you arrived. I had notes of your flight. I had Perkins's address. They could take it all from there.'

'It's fantastic. I don't see what there was to gain. I mean I had nothing in my documents to help anyone. I just don't believe that there can be a connection.'

'I do.' His voice was flat, hard. 'Someone wanted those gold shares, Tim. For some reason we don't know about.'

'Then why attack me? If they'd broken into your office, they knew I hadn't got them.'

His voice went down to a mutter. 'That's what Maguire says. Exactly the same. I'll test that theory somehow. I'll test it.'

'Andy! For heaven's sake! Leave it to the cops.'

'You're a fine one to talk. You never would. Not if it was your client. Not if you felt responsible.'

That silenced me. I held the phone without speaking until he came back to me again, his voice more conciliatory in tone. 'Look, Tim, I guess I'm kind of wound up over this. I'll call you again soon. Keep me posted on your movements. All right?'

'All right, Andy. Try not to dwell on it. And for heaven's sake let the police deal with it.'

He rang off. I sat in my hotel room and smiled a wry smile at my advice to him, advice I'd never taken myself. I hoped he wouldn't upset Maguire in the way that I have upset Nobby Roberts, my old Scotland Yard friend, in the past. Maguire might not be so tolerant; he and Andy might be involved with the same Catholic church, but that was hardly the same as having played rugger together, like Nobby and me, now was it? Work that one out, if you can.

Carlton was very cooperative for the next two days. I got all the facts I needed. From time to time he or Howarth would appear beside me, nod hopefully, and push off without interfering. I took taxis to and from my hotel and worked in my room at night. I didn't really have time to reflect that I was wasting the entire facilities for entertainment of the greatest city in the world for diversions; I had too much to do. Sue began to make noises on the telephone that indicated that now she had caught up with all her old girlfriends during my absence, and done the things that she claims my presence prevents her from doing, she was getting bored and it was time I was back. She did give instructions that I was to go to a couple of exhibitions in New York on her behalf and get catalogues; art catalogues, of course. I decided on the morning of the third day that I'd got all I needed for the moment; I could do the number-crunching back home. I told Carlton and Howarth that I would catch an evening flight back to London.

'Finished already? What's the verdict?'

'The jury is still out. I'll tell you the result after I've got back.'

'Infuriating fellow. After you've seen Jeremy, I suppose?'

'Of course.'

'Well, do your best for us.' Howarth looked serious. 'I'm more and more convinced that we must expand, and expand quickly.'

'I'll work as fast as I can.'

'What are you doing this afternoon?'

'Some shopping. Then I'm going to the Metropolitan.'

'Really? What to see?'

'I'm getting a catalogue for Sue. Then I'll look in on

the Rodin section. The Art Fund owns a terracotta by him of Gwen John. The Met has some studies in plaster for the Whistler memorial. One of them is unmistakably her. I want to look at it. See how it compares.'

Carlton, standing next to Howarth, nodded. 'I remember them. I'm sure you're right. Is that your full programme, then?'

'That and the Whitney. I'm under orders to see that.'

'Ah, the Whitney.' He gave me a long, owlish stare. 'An excellent exhibition. Is that a particular interest?'

'Well, yes, but mainly to Sue. She wants the catalogue.'

He nodded again. 'It's a good one. Lots of detail. Well, I'm sure we'll be in touch.'

'When will you be in England again?'

He gave me a rather surprised look and glanced quickly at Howarth. 'For the next board meeting, without doubt. Assuming, that is, that we'll have your report and be taking a decision to go ahead on Chicago?'

Chapter Eight

I was up and dressed before she was, rooting myself out a reasonable breakfast and setting it, together with her coffee, on the table next to the long window that overlooks Onslow Gardens. The autumn sun had the gardens all lit up with amber and rust above the green grass across the road, making me feel glad to be back for the time of year that is London's very best. I had spent the day before at the Bank, because modern flights get into Heathrow in the morning and Sue had already gone to the Tate when I got clear of the airport. Jeremy was away at a conference of brokers for the day, so I'd worked undisturbed until evening, when I returned to take Sue out to a trattoria round the corner before an early night. She came out of the bedroom wearing my thick white towelling robe wrapped round her, freshly showered she was, slightly tousled and healthy and delicious to look at above her bare feet and slender ankles. It gave me a pang of regret that I'd bothered to get up and get dressed.

'I think I can safely say,' she said, throwing her head back in a grandly masculine gesture as she sat down to her coffee with a nod of approval, so that I knew she was letting me have a quote, not a statement of her own, 'that without a single exception, the partners of my pleasure have either been charmed by my evident superiority or completely paralysed by the vigour of my performance.'

I had a mouthful of tea in place at the time she said

it, and it went down so skew that it nearly came back all over the table. When I had finished coughing and spluttering I looked up to see her shrewd blue eyes resting on me sardonically and meaningfully with that mockery that women nowadays show for a man's conceit.

'Sue, really!' I heaved another painful cough and wiped my mouth. 'Really! I don't think that I have ever – I mean – I'm sure, not even when thoroughly plastered, have I ever uttered such a – a – '

'Chauvinistic?' She smiled sweetly.

'Well, yes, but not so much chauvinistic perhaps, but such a – a – self-satisfied – I – well – paralysed is hardly the word I would have – '

'You didn't.'

'Eh?'

'You didn't. Say it. I wasn't quoting you.' She smiled at my discomfiture. Women can be like that, especially after a night of – of – no, I won't risk saying it.

'You weren't?'

'No. I wasn't.'

Relief flooded through me. Tim Simpson may have his faults but, despite an attraction to the ladies, he doesn't say things it wouldn't be gallant to . . . Well, there may have been times when I've felt a bit, what, *pleased* with events perhaps, but I wouldn't, I mean, I really wouldn't . . . I gaped at her.

'Then who the hell did? Where on earth did you get a statement like that from? Eh?'

'Moreton Frewen.'

'What?'

She lifted her coffee cup, utterly composed. 'You mean who. Moreton Frewen. He wrote it in his diary in later life. He was a real Victorian hunting man of the old school. I rather think he felt that the ladies were in luck when he was about.'

'Men should never keep diaries. They – Hey! Wait a minute! What do you mean? How the hell – how have you been reading Moreton Frewen's diary?'

She shook her head as she buttered a piece of toast. 'I haven't. Been reading his diary. Or diaries. I have been reading Anita Leslie. Boning up on Moreton Frewen. I have read – '

'Oh no! Now look here, Sue – '

'I have read – ' she put down the toast and began ticking them off on her fingers – 'Anita Leslie's book, *Mr Frewen of England*, which is straight biography. I have read *The Fabulous Leonard Jerome*, he was the father-in-law, then *Jennie*, then *My Cousin Clare* – she was Moreton Frewen's daughter, Clare Sheridan, quite a life that was, Charlie Chaplin and Trotsky and F. E. Smith, you name them, the quote came from that one – then I read *Edwardians in Love* and then – '

'Suc! Stop it! Stop it at once!'

'Then I read Ralph Martin's *Lady Randolph Churchill* – my goodness, those Society beauties didn't half have a life, Tim, she was Jennie Jerome, you know, Winston's mother, she had a succession of – '

'I know! I know! For Christ's sake! I know who Jennie Jerome was! I – '

'What on earth is the matter with you?' She bit a piece of toast off very crisply and cocked her head on one side. 'You look quite congested. Not at all as relaxed as you were when you got up. What's wrong?'

I ground my napkin up into a ball on the table. 'You know very well what's wrong! You're – you're getting involved, damn it!'

'Why? Shouldn't I? Don't you want me to help?'

There was a look of casual unconcern about her, a gentle interest only, as though the question was totally unimportant. I recognized it. Pure gelignite. Absolutely lethal peril. I knew that look too well. This was thin ice, rapid quicksand, hot coals, the Niagaran tightrope, walking across the greenhouse roof in hob-nailed boots. Very light treading was called for.

'Um, no, of course, I mean, any assistance is always gratefully received. Most appreciated. It's just that I – well – I wouldn't like you to, er, to waste your time, that's all. Knowing how busy you are, and all that.'

She smiled. Prickles went down the back of my neck. 'Dear Tim. So considerate. Surely you should know that a woman's greatest pleasure is to help the man of her dreams?'

'Oh my God.' I put my head in my hands. This was going to be much worse than expected.

'I mean, it surely must be helpful to get to know one's subject in detail? Like Moreton Frewen and his contacts? The fact that he was one of Lillie Langtry's earliest beaux? The question of those gold shares? I know they're only of marginal importance to you and Andy Casey, but he is an old friend, isn't he?'

'Yes, Sue.'

'And you'd like to help him?'

'Yes, Sue.'

'And the story of Frewen's gold-crusher, for instance; that might be relevant?'

'Yes, Sue.'

'You knew about the gold-crusher?'

'Yes, Sue.'

'And the other mining ventures?'

'I – er – well, some of them.'

'They could be relevant?'

'Yes, Sue.'

'And I mean there's no harm, is there, in my reading up a lot of harmless old books while you're away, just in case something useful might turn up, just to help you? To pass the long hours of your absence?'

'No, Sue.'

'And I mean it's not as though there's any danger, is there, like there was with the Whistler or the Norman Shaw thing this year, nothing criminal or violent or anything?'

'No, Sue.' I shot a hopeless glance out of the window. The punch was coming from a mile back, I knew it, there was nothing to stop it, nothing.

'In that case – ' her teeth flashed now, as she slapped her cup back into the saucer and leant across the table with her beautiful blue eyes narrowed into scowling slits – 'why are you so upset about my interest? Why? More important, why is there the trace of a substantial bruise on the right side of your face, across most of the lower jaw? Why?'

'Oh.' I involuntarily put a hand to the place where the lumber-jacket had belted me one. Morning sunlight is so much more revealing than evening lamplight. 'Oh, that. Oh, nothing. Just an accident.'

'Really? An accident? Don't tell me: you ran into a bus?'

'No.'

'You took on Marvin Hagler?'

'No. Now look – '

'Witherspoon?'

'Sue. This is quite – '

'Someone's husband caught you?'

'Sue, really! That's in poor taste!'

Her mouth drew into a humorous line. 'All right. I'll withdraw that. I won't withdraw the suspicion of criminal violence.' She held up a finger. 'Don't speak! I know you, Tim Simpson. I know you. I knew when you left Donald White's. I knew it. I could feel it in my bones. There's going to be trouble over this, I thought, big trouble. There you were with that look on your face, all innocent and eager and wide-eyed, while Donald warned you. Just like a little boy. It sent a chill right through me. There's another one coming, I thought, another nasty violent chase after something long dead, something that should stay dead and buried, but he won't leave it, not Tim, that's not my Tim, assuming he is my Tim. He couldn't. And you know what I've told you before; either I'm part of it and I join in and help you and keep you out of more trouble than you'll get into on your own, let alone with other women, or I'm leaving. Right now. So make up your mind. There has been trouble, hasn't there?'

'Jesus Christ. I got mugged at the airport. Just an attempted mugging. So stop behaving like something from an Italian opera.'

'Pah!'

'I have to go to work. To the office. I'm going now.'

'You certainly are not! Not until you've told me!'

'There is nothing to tell.'

'Pah! Come on: cough it up.'

There's nothing you can do with Sue when she's in one of these moods. Absolutely nothing. She has that teacher-type quality that makes you feel like a recalcitrant prep-schoolboy caught with a large sticky toffee in the side of his mouth during a lesson on Religious Practice. You're never quite sure whether you've got a chance of surreptitiously swallowing the evidence or whether you'll have to bring it out on to the table top, all gooey and slimy and utterly disgusting. Either way, you know you're not going to get away with it. I stared gloomily at the charming cleavage where my bath robe had fallen open at the neck as she leant at me over the breakfast table. She sat quickly back and pulled the lapels tight up to her throat.

'That's enough of that! Come on – speak up! What happened?'

I sighed, replenished my tea and gave her a steady synopsis of everything that had taken place in Chicago, keeping it fairly brief. At the end of it I realized she was sitting absolutely still, with her eyes closed.

'Dear God,' she said.

'I'll get you some more coffee if you like.'

'No.' She held up her hand. 'Not yet. This is terrible. Much worse than I'd imagined.'

'Oh, come on, Sue.'

'Is there nothing – absolutely nothing – that you can do to avoid this sort of thing?'

'Sue, really.'

'I mean, could you not have let them have your case? No – no, I'm sorry. Of course you couldn't. They'd have – it wouldn't have made any difference. And that poor man. Thank God I wasn't there this time.'

'Yes.'

'Tim, you can't really believe that the mugging at the airport and the break-in at Andy's and the murder of that poor man weren't all connected?'

'Oh, come on, Sue, for heaven's sake! They might be, but they might not.'

'Pah! Of course they were. And the gold-mine shares have all gone?'

'It seems like it.'

'Who did you tell that you were going to see Andy about those shares before you left?'

'What, here? In England?'

Her mouth puckered. 'Yes, here. In England.'

'Look, Sue, everything that has happened has happened in America. It has nothing to do with people here. Nothing. There's no reason.'

'Then why did they go for you? You specifically. As soon as you got off the plane? Why?'

She was voicing suspicions I'd already had, suspicions I'd pushed to the back of my mind as unwelcome and disturbing. There was no future in that line of thought.

'If they knew Andy had asked me for information then they'd naturally be in wait for me. I'm sure the source of it all is in the States, Sue. Not here in England.'

She tapped the side of her cup impatiently with a teaspoon. 'Who?'

I sighed. 'Jeremy, of course. One or two people at the Bank. The board of Christerby's. Donald. More than a few people at his party, who were listening.'

'That's hopeless! You might just as well have put a megaphone at the top of Bishopsgate and let the entire City of London know. Really, Tim!'

I felt my hackles rising. I'd had enough of this. There are limits to what I'll take. I leant forward over the table. 'There was no reason to be furtive about it, you know. It was all quite open and above board. I've had enough of this guilt-transference bit. A man owned some old shares, had good title to them, and wanted a bit of information about a previous owner, long dead. There was no breach of confidentiality. None. There's no need to act as though I'd broken the Official Secrets Act, damn it.' I got up suddenly.

I needed air. 'I did nothing to attract violence that could possibly have been foreseen! You sit there all bloody smug and I-told-you-so as though you or anyone else could have made the slightest difference! Or behaved differently.'

'All right, all right! Don't shout at me.'

'I will shout at you! I'm fed up with this! It'll be bad enough having Jeremy put on his Scottish-Elder-of-the-Kirk expression of woe when I get to the Bank today without having you take me through a set of preliminary accusations. I thought you were on my side.'

'Tim! I am! Oh, I am! Can't you see that?' She flung herself upwards out of the chair and grabbed me as I turned angrily away. 'I'm trying to help. Please, Tim; you came home last night and you didn't tell me anything. You weren't going to, either, were you? How can I help and be close to you if you won't tell me? I've had to wring it out of you.' Her mouth trembled slightly. 'You're not fair!'

'I don't want you in danger. I know – I've said I don't believe there's any part of it over here, it's an American thing, but I don't want any risk, any sort of risk at all. I don't want you involved, like before. It's been too dangerous, and I'm superstitious because of the mention of Brighton.'

She shook her head sadly and held me, a little less tightly, but not letting me go, putting her face close to mine so that I had to look at her right there, her breath smelling of coffee and her body of soap and damp towelling.

'You'll never learn, will you? I want to be with you and to look after you.'

'You? Look after me?'

'Yes. Me. Look after you. I have terrible fears

about what might happen to you if I'm not there. You need a guardian angel, Tim. Try and think of me as that. Oh, of course I can't cope with violence or anything, but we work so well together and I – well – I can stop you rushing in where you shouldn't. No, don't look at me like that. You've had a lot of luck, Tim, a lot of luck. When I was away in Australia there was that woman and you got shot. One day, your luck'll run out. You're quick and strong and you never seem to be afraid; you've got such a temper when you're threatened, you don't seem to think of what could happen. I suppose that's what stops other people; they think of the danger and hesitate. If someone doesn't do that for you, one day it'll be too – Something dreadful will happen.'

How strange, I thought, her eyes have filled with tears and she's worried about me, as though I can't look after myself, when all the world knows it would be she who would be in danger. My friends would never forgive me if anything happened to her, never mind what I would feel. No one worries about me, I can handle myself, but my actions bring danger to her. How strange.

'I'm sorry, Sue.' I kissed her gently. 'Of course I know. I'm sorry. I'll tell you everything about this one, really I will. There won't be anything more to bother about over here, though. It'll be Andy Casey and the Chicago PD who'll bear the brunt this time. Really.'

She smiled uncertainly. 'I wish I could believe you.'

'It's true. Really it is. I must get to the Bank, Sue. I'm late already.'

She let go of me. 'Go carefully, Tim. Please go carefully.'

'Of course I will. Cheer up; we'll go out somewhere nice this evening, perhaps the theatre? What d'you say?'

'That would be great. But please, Tim, leave off chasing after any gold shares, will you?'

'Of course I will. And you can leave all those books on Moreton Frewen alone. We won't need any more information about Moreton Frewen. You can bet on that.'

Chapter Nine

Jeremy White clasped his hands to his blond head in a dramatic gesture. It irritated me. I don't know if you've noticed, but people always behave with mock drama when you least want them to. Perhaps age is making me irascible, but I wasn't in the mood for another session on a cross-Atlantic view of events in Chicago, not after the one I'd had with Sue already that morning.

'My dear Tim! For the Good Lord's sake! Can *nothing* be done to – to – '

'Keep me out of trouble?'

'Precisely! Perfectly put. You go dashing about the world, barging into these situations with such predictable vigour. Couldn't you possibly have managed, just for once, to avoid this sort of thing?'

'They tried to pinch my bags.'

'Why you? Eh? Why your bags? Why not someone else's bags? Can you answer me that?'

'No.'

'I mean, you can't treat a place like Chicago as though Al Capone was still running around, you know. Tim, this is nineteen eighty-six.'

'Jeremy – '

'It isn't as though you couldn't make an effort of some kind to be normal, respectable. Do you have to fly into airports with fists bunched, bashing out left, right and centre – '

'Jeremy,' I roared, standing up and shoving my face right into his, 'who was it that made me go to

Chicago? Eh? I didn't bloody well want to go, but you insisted – yes, you – you made me go post-haste because of your typical desire to shove your nose into Christerby's business. Everything that happened happened because of you, not me!'

He sat back in his desk chair, startled, my face within inches of his, my body arched over his desk in a furious curve that stretched me so far that, fortunately, I couldn't reach any further. I'm very fond of Jeremy in many ways, but at that moment I could quite cheerfully have pasted him one.

'My dear Tim! There's no need to behave like this! Really! I make a mild criticism, the merest gentle reproof, suggest that you might take greater precautions, comport yourself more calmly, and you go right off the deep end! I sometimes wonder, you know, whether all these imbroglios you get into aren't having an effect. You're behaving like someone entirely *unhinged*.'

I opened my mouth, fairly wide, and then closed it again. Then I backed and sat down in the chair which I had just vacated, across the desk from him. We glared at each other unflinchingly. After a while he swallowed, opened his mouth, closed it and buzzed his secretary.

'We'd better have coffee,' he said. 'I'm not sure that you'd better not have a brandy with yours.'

I didn't answer. Words were quite useless.

'There's no need to sulk.'

'I am not sulking!'

'All right! All right. There's no need to shout, either. Coffee, thank you, yes.' He waited until his secretary left the room. 'You've absolutely terrified her. I've never seen her roll her eyes like that before.'

I managed to resist telling him that the eye-rolling

had been in sympathy with me. Jeremy's secretaries know all too well what coping with him is like. He got up, went to his side-cabinet, got out two glasses, poured a liberal dose of Rémy Martin into each, handed me one and took a swig of his own just as his secretary came in and put down a tray of coffee. She gave us a significant second roll of her eyes and went out again. I drank a stimulating sip and felt a soothing fire purge through me.

'Brandy at eleven in the morning,' said Jeremy, suddenly cheerful. 'With coffee. Just like Spain? My Uncle Richard often had a split of champagne for his elevenses, you know. Said it was very good for you. I'm not sure I don't prefer a nip of brandy myself. Better for you.'

'Churchill thought so.'

'Ah, Churchill. And what of his uncle? The improvident Moreton Frewen?'

'Nothing new, really. Well, that's not quite true. Andy Casey knew quite a bit about him. From the cattle business. The Powder River ranch.'

'The what?' Jeremy was suddenly alert, coffee in one hand, glass in the other.

'The Powder River ranch. Where the Frewens ranched, in Wyoming.'

'Good God!' He nearly spilled his coffee. 'Of course! Hugh Lowther. The Yellow Earl!'

'What?'

'I'd completely forgotten. I heard that story at Eton.'

'What story?'

He stared at me. 'Haven't you read *The Yellow Earl* by Douglas Sutherland?'

'No, I can't say I have. What is it?'

'It's the story of Hugh Lowther, the Earl of Lons-dale. The boxer. You've heard of the Lonsdale Belt?'

'Of course.'

'Well, that was Hugh Lowther. He was a pal of Frewen's. Risked his inheritance to put money into the Powder River Cattle Company. It's a glorious story. Lowther took his wife Grace with him when he went hunting with Frewen on the ranch. One day when they were out in the wilds shooting, someone told them that a dreadful bandit and horse thief, called Little Henry, had been seen heading for the ranch house, where they'd left Grace Lowther alone with a female companion. This Little Henry was a notorious murderer. Frewen and Lowther were hor-rified; they drew their guns and galloped the whole way back to Frewen Castle, as it was called. They found Little Henry sitting in the living-room, having tea with Grace Lowther.' Jeremy started to laugh. 'It turned out that he'd been at Eton with Hugh.'

'He was an Old Etonian?'

'Absolutely. He was shot dead later, by Bat Master-son, in Dodge City.' He chuckled. 'You should read that book. Lowther was good with his fists; he knocked out the odd cowboy here and there.' He straightened his face. 'Look, I'm sorry if I was a bit of a bore just now, Tim.'

'Of course you weren't. I'm sorry if I was a bit touchy. I had Sue on the subject earlier and it ruffled the feathers a bit.'

He smiled and put down his empty glass. 'Good. That's all over then. Now, let's hear all about Chris-terby's. I suppose they've convinced you that Chicago is essential?'

'Not quite. Here, let's go through these figures.' I

slapped a sheaf of papers on his desk. 'There's a few aspects we have to discuss before I finalize my report.'

That was it. With Jeremy the changes are abrupt, and rancour never exists. He expects vigorous action and he behaves vigorously himself. The worst thing you can do when handling Jeremy is to be weak; he discounts weak people entirely. What he likes is high fettle, high spirits, no compromise. As long as you retain your nerve you can always deal with Jeremy. We plunged into the figures I'd assembled and he was alarmingly positive; after a while I could tell he'd grasped the essentials completely. There were still some bits of the picture that needed more work and we agreed to meet again to finish the whole thing.

'Excellent,' he said. 'My congratulations to Andy, and this fellow Carlton. Seems to have been very helpful. I'm off to lunch; sorry, I can't join you. One last thing.' He gave me a careful look. 'There's nothing more to do on this gold shares business, is there?'

'Nothing, Jeremy.'

'I mean, I'm sorry for Andy. Nasty business. But we're not involved?'

'Not at all. I mean, I never met Perkins. Never saw the shares. Andy is the one who's landed with all that.'

He heaved a sigh of relief. 'Thank heavens. With you safely back here, there can't be any more repercussions. It's a matter for Chicago. Well, I'm off. Keep me posted if there's any more news.'

'Right.'

He strode out, head up, leaving me to collect my papers and trot back to my office. His secretary gave me a wink as I passed. The business of the Bank was going on all around me, normal and grave, as any financial institution likes to appear, remote from the fisticuffs of Chicago, the art barter of New York and the bustle of Bond Street. I decided to work through lunch, and was deeply immersed in various erudite computations when, early in the afternoon, Andy Casey called me from Chicago.

'Andy! Hello. How are you?'

'Those stocks were worthless.' His voice was clipped.

'What?' I reared up behind the phone like a startled giraffe.

'Those gold stocks of Perkins's. For the mines in Utah and Colorado and Dakota. A letter came in from the specialist he'd sent the list to. Frank, his son, phoned to tell me. I made him read the list out and you can bet I've had it checked. Every damn item on it.'

'Worthless?' A stab of hopeful delight went through me.

'Absolutely. The mines they all relate to have been worked out for years. Companies have been wound up or defunct in some way. They have no value as mine stocks.'

'None? Are you sure?'

'None. They're just paper, Tim. Printed paper. The specialist says they have low value as collector's items, too. As a documentary record, some college might like them. For maybe a thousand bucks. No more.' He sighed, a long, deep sigh that brought the weariness of his condition all the way down a few thousand miles of telephone line. 'Maybe the University in Laramie or somewhere might like them. I thought we had something there. Our researchers found that a guy called Wood of Mobil Oil donated a pile of Frewen's papers to the University in Laramie. It seems a lot of English and Scots upper crust first ranched Wyoming as well as Frewen. Moncrieffes, Wallops – Lord Portsmouth – there were quite a crowd. But that's just history. That's all we here at OMC came up with: History.' His voice sounded disgusted. 'I just can't believe it. That people would murder poor old Perkins for worthless paper. I just can't believe it; it doesn't make sense.'

I spoke back cautiously, because I wanted to break out into a shriek of joy, but Andy was still upset and I felt for him, felt sorry for his distress because it's a situation I've found myself in before and it hurt me to see Andy in the same state. 'At least we had the luck that Perkins had put a specialist on to the shares before he was murdered and they were stolen. We might have gone on guessing for ever.'

'True. We have to be glad about that.' He sounded about as glad as the last man to cross the line in the Derby. 'I just can't accept it. It's so meaningless. So random.'

'What does Maguire say, now?'

'He says it confirms what they thought. That there was no connection between your attack, our break-in and Perkins's death. The murder is just another statistic to them. I can understand that. Maguire says if you knew what some of these crooks murder for, you wouldn't be sceptical. They murder for anything, for the hope of a few bucks. Well, he's a policeman. I don't believe it this time.'

'Andy, come on; don't let it get to you. It was a terrible thing, an awful thing, but it was one of those violent events you read about every day. It doesn't make it any better or more acceptable, but that's the way these things go.'

'I just can't accept it.' His voice was dogged. 'I'm not going to let it rest.'

'Now you're following a bad example. A very bad example.'

'Yours.'

'Exactly. It'll do you no good. Go home; go and play golf; try to leave the office for a day and get over it a bit. There's nothing you can do. It's over. It's another burglary murder statistic. Leave it to the police. Please?'

There was silence for a moment. 'I hear you, Tim. I hear you. But I'm not convinced. I'll give you a call in a day or two. OK?'

'OK. But please try to relax. The police will deal with it. One way or the other.'

He put the phone down. I didn't exactly dance round the office, because it isn't big enough, but I did leap to my feet and caper round my desk in unholy joy. Pure, unadulterated joy. There was no connection with me; the gold shares were worthless; it wasn't worth any planned, coordinated series of attacks; it was all random, unconnected. I pranced out and got two theatre tickets. I left a note on Jeremy's desk. I worked like lightning all afternoon and then I rushed out and bought a big bunch of flowers. Back at Onslow Gardens I presented the big bunch to Sue and hugged her delighted body to me to make up for the bad start to the morning. I swept her to the theatre and I took her to dinner. I laid it on with a trowel. There was music. There was atmosphere. We went to a night club. We drank champagne. We taxied back after two o'clock in a happy daze of romantic anticipation. I paid off the taxi and practically carried Sue up the stairs to the door of the flat, feeling her warm and soft and completely receptive in my arms.

The front door was open.

They had jemmied open the mortice lock with savage disregard for woodwork and paint. Splintered edges hung from the architrave.

They had gone through the flat like a whirlwind, opening, overturning, knocking down, wrenching apart.

They had left the paintings on the walls, the Clarkson Stanfield over the fireplace, the Seago and the Spencer Gore, the John etching of Dorelia, all the lady artists that Sue collects.

They had torn all the drawers open, the desk, the side cabinet, the newspaper rack. The kitchen looked as though a bomb had hit it and the bedroom looked as though it had taken the force of the blast.

They had pulled books out of the big bookcase on the wall, spilling them all over, hurling them, trampling them. There was one particular pile, separate from the rest, that Sue, cold and stiff and white, walked over to and knelt beside. It seemed as though the intruders had concentrated on that particular pile. They were shaken, ripped open, spreadeagled, hurled aside and re-scoured, as though the violator had been madly seeking some unimaginable inconceivable secret within them, contained on a slip of paper, a bookmark, a notation of some kind. Sue looked up from the pile. Her lips were thin and tight, like the voice that came from them.

'All these books are Anita Leslie's on the Frewens and the Jeromes. Don't tell me now – ' her voice rose a pitch – 'don't tell me ever again, that this is all a coincidence. Pure coincidence. Only to do with America, you said? Nothing to do with you at all?'

Chapter Ten

'Sporting, military and thespian specialities,' said Mr Goodston, smiling amiably at me over his half-moon spectacles. 'You know me, Mr Simpson.' He waved a plump arm in the direction of the dusty shelves around him, almost knocking over a teetering pile of books, one of several stacked on the desk in front of him. 'What is to be our pleasure this time?' His chair creaked as he sat back, revealing a stained and bulging checked waistcoat under his sagging corduroy jacket.

His Praed Street bookshop, just round the corner from Paddington Station, looks small when you go in, clogged with ranks and piles of gloomily subfusc bindings, only alleviated by the occasional bright jacket. Not much of Mr Goodston's stock is of recent origin. I rather suspect that he regards anything produced since 1945 as needing time to assess, like a port that has not been sufficiently mellowed. Only now and again does he have to accede to modern biography, memoirs of aged, retired generals and similar rather immature vintages. The shop is deceptive, because I happen to know that the floors above are also loaded with ancient volumes, valuable many of them, carefully preserved under lock and key, behind glass for the really rare ones, not accessible to the public. I don't know why he has always been so friendly to me, so helpful and encouraging. Perhaps it is because the younger generation are not prominent among his clients, particularly the collectors rather than dealers, and he likes the idea, the concept of my building up a collection over, say, the next forty years, in the manner of nineteenth-century bibliophiles. He is a cautious, fat man of great professionalism and wisdom, so in a sense he flatters me by his encouragement. Perhaps that is part of his selling style; pandering to one's conceit.

'It will be a thespian matter again, I suppose? Ellen Terry perhaps, or did I provide you with sufficient material on her and her, um, companion, Mr Godwin, the last time?' He smiled a knowing smile. 'And Gordon Craig? I've never really felt a permanent enthusiasm for the theatre in you, Mr Simpson, though, I must say. It must be nearly a couple of years since you seemed to be so keen on Ellen Terry and her, um, associations. Is it something theatrical this time?'

I grinned at him. He'd diverted me from the first question I was going to ask and alerted me to something parallel, a subject which might draw something of interest from him.

'Not really, Mr Goodston, unless, of course, you include Lillie Langtry among your thespian treasures?'

His eyebrows shot up. His half-lights slipped a little further down his nose. 'Lillie Langtry! Good heavens! Of course I do. My goodness.' He waved his plump arm grandiloquently about him. 'The Jersey Lily. She is to be found, I may say, ubiquitously among these shelves. She got about a bit, Mr Simpson my dear young man, she got about a bit, as they say, quite apart from her celebrated er, association with his Royal, er, Majesty, Edward the Seventh.' He chuckled rumbustiously. 'Sporting, military *and* thespian specialities, ha-ha. She figures in all of 'em, my boy, all of 'em. My advice to you is to specialize. Otherwise you'll be buying up a major portion of my stock.'

'Come, come, Mr Goodston, that's a bit ungallant. As it happens, my interest is sporting, rather than military or thespian.'

'Understandable, sir, from a distinguished Rugby blue like yourself, but – '

'No, Mr Goodston. Not rugger. Hunting is my interest on this occasion. Fox-hunting. The Quorn, the Spottesmore, all that. Lillie Langtry was a, what shall I say, frequent guest at hunting parties. I have come to you as the oracle on the subject.'

He inclined his head gracefully. For all his other interests, I happen to know that Mr Goodston has a passion for fox-hunting memoirs, old racing books, legends of the Turf. Most of Mr Goodston's profits, if there are any, go into the betting shop across the road. He is a veteran punter. When Mr Goodston's shop is closed you know that there is a major meeting on somewhere, the jumps or the flat, it makes no difference. Mr Goodston is a racing man.

'Actually, what I came to ask you was a specific thing. A specific book. It's called *Melton Mowbray and Other Memories*. By a man called Moreton Frewen. Herbert Jenkins, 1924. You haven't got a copy, by any chance?'

There was a silence. Very slowly, he took off his half-lights and put them down on the desk in front of him. He sat forward and peered at me for a moment, giving rise to an uneasy feeling in me that I had asked for something forbidden, something accessible normally only to a secret coterie.

'Moreton Frewen,' he murmured. 'My goodness. Moreton Frewen.'

'It seems, Mr Goodston, that he was one of Lillie Langtry's earlier beaux. Among others. He and his future brother-in-law, John Leslie, took her riding in the Park.'

'Jack Leslie,' he corrected gently, almost absent-mindedly. 'They called him Jack. Shy fellow, Irish baronet. She fell off Frewen's park hack, Redskin, into Leslie's arms.' A smile came to his face. 'Part of her technique, they used to say. Falling into swoons, I mean. When a suitable gentleman's arms were available, of course. But good heavens! no one has asked me for a Frewen book for years. Not for years.'

'Do you have one?'

He gave me a reproachful glance. Picking up his comic spectacles, he put them on, hoisted himself to his feet and moved cautiously out from behind his desk. His bulk puttered along the shelves behind him and disappeared behind a sagging wall of loaded bookcases. The voice that came out from behind this bibliophilic screen was ruminative, philosophical, nostalgic.

'Melton Mowbray,' it said. 'Melton Mowbray. Jenkins. A green book, or rather, greeny-blue in the classic Herbert Jenkins design. Are you a reader of P. G. Wodehouse, Mr Simpson?'

'Of course. All true Englishmen are.'

'Then the book pattern will be familiar to you. Unmistakable Herbert Jenkins, long gone now, of course. Why, here we are. Melton Mowbray.'

He spoke the words lovingly, as though he were cutting keenly through the crispy crust of one of those renowned pork pies with a boiled egg in the centre, that carries the name of that celebrated hunting town. An eponymous pork pie, I thought humorously, of a type to which I am very much drawn. Mr Goodston, however, had emerged from his book-lined dug-out and was holding the volume under my nose, showing, sure enough, the well-known design with its black border line that any P. G. Wodehouse collector would instantly recognize. With a smile of triumph he opened it carefully, retaining it out of reach of my grasp, to show me a photograph of a party in hunting clothes standing posed outside the front door of a country house. 'A Hunting Party at Quenby Hall, Melton Mowbray,' he quoted, from the title under it. 'The tall, straight young man in white riding breeches on the right is Moreton Frewen. Next to him, seated, Lord Manners. On his left, seated, Mrs Langtry.' He smiled gently. 'Sporting, military, and thespian specialities. He introduced her to his future father-in-law in New York, you know. In the company of Oscar Wilde. Jerome was a connoisseur of fine women. Lent her his famous railway carriage to tour in. Frewen met her at Cheyenne and gave a party for her. A gala night.'

'People must have been very broad-minded in those days.'

He smiled secretly. 'Discreet. Discreet is the word you're looking for. The copy is fine. Yours for fifteen pounds.'

'Done.'

'Thank you kindly. Got all you need?'

'Oh yes. This will complete it, what with the Leslie books.'

He gave me a reproving stare. 'When you say you've read all the Leslie and Jerome and Churchill books, I take it that you mean you've got all the Anita Leslie ones?'

'Yes. Yes, that's it.'

'You didn't buy them from me.'

'No. Er, no. Sue, my girlfriend; she got them.'

'Humph. What about this then?' Triumphantly, he swept another small book into view, a hardback with a dust wrapper depicting a man in a bowler hat staring out directly under a title. 'The Splendid Pauper,' he chirruped. 'Allen Andrews. It was Harrap over here but this is the Lippincott edition, New York, 1968. Have you read it? Have you got it?'

'No. No, I haven't.'

'This is good. Better, from your point of view. More detailed than Anita Leslie's; more factual. She was his great-niece, after all, so she was emotionally involved, and she was an Irish Leslie, so you tend to get quite a lot of the Irish aspect of things from her. Andrews is better on the business aspects; I'm sure you'll know that Ralph Martin, in his book on Lady Randolph Churchill, says as much. Anita Leslie didn't bother with the detail of the businesses so much. Being a woman she probably found them less interesting, or maybe they were hard to grasp. She's very readable, of course, a good writer, but not a modern biographer. Between the two of them, you'll get most of the story, most of it that matters, anyway. Oddly enough, both she and Andrews died last year, so you won't be able to consult them.'

I nodded respectfully. 'I understand. I know she does go on a bit about Ireland. It's a bit like Elizabeth Longford on Wellington. Both she and Anita Leslie had a particular axe to grind in that direction. We all tend to think of it as part of the background, not relevant to the real story.'

He gave me a long, hard stare, holding the book firmly, as though reluctant to hand it over to me. His eyes became severe. 'My very dear young man, let me give you a piece of advice before you jump to hasty conclusions on either of those two lady authors. Whenever you are delving into the past – or the present – history or situation of the British Isles, never, but never, neglect what I call the Irish Dimension. Never. It is a fatal mistake.' He pushed his glasses back up his nose and modified the stare, mellowing it down a bit. 'Would you like me to tell you a story about Frewen, to illustrate the point?'

I nodded as gracefully as my impatient urge to snatch the book off him would allow. 'Please do.'

He beamed happily. 'Frewen's mother was Anglo-Irish, a Homan from County Kildare. It may account for the fact that her four sons were as wild as March hares. Frewen, who was a Sussex Englishman, sat in Parliament as MP for East Cork, but gave the seat back to Tim Healy. His nephew Shane Leslie – ' he pronounced it not as in the cowboy film, *Shane*, but in the Irish way, Sean or Shawn – 'Anita's father, became a Catholic and espoused the Republican cause, despite an Anglo-Irish baronet father and an American Protestant mother, Leonie Jerome.'

'I see. A bit complicated – '

'I haven't finished yet.'

'Sorry.'

'Frewen's brother Stephen, the Lancer Colonel, had a daughter called Ruby. Moreton tried to get her to marry a rich Jewish man so that the wealth would bale out the family fortune, decimated by Moreton, and de-mortgage the family home, Brickwall in Sussex. Ruby refused and, when he hounded her, she married someone else.'

I realized I had been given a cue. 'Who?'

'Carson.'

'Carson? Sir Edward Carson? Wilde's prosecutor?'

'The very same. Carson of Ulster. So Carson had a

double reason to distrust Frewen. There in the same family, you see, you have a bankrupt English gentleman with an Irish estate at Innishannon, near Cork; a Catholic convert Republican hereditary Irish baronet; and a rabid Ulster secessionist Protestant leader. A classic Irish triangle. Never neglect the Irish Dimension, dear sir, never. Do you follow my drift?'

'I do,' I said humbly. 'I do. Please may I see that book?'

'You may.' He handed it over. 'I would suggest that it is indispensable. It is in very good condition. It will cost you five pounds. *The Splendid Pauper*. The story of Moreton Frewen, by Allen Andrews.'

'Done.'

'Wise fellow.'

I held the book in front of me, barring his way for a moment. 'Tell me – why is it that you are so knowledgeable about Frewen? What prompted this encyclopaedic interest?'

His eyes flicked slyly at me. 'You mock me, Mr Simpson.'

'No, no! I assure you. You quote chapter and verse, detailed family knowledge. How come?'

He smiled and took his glasses off again. A distant look came into his face. 'You're not a betting man? A gambler of any kind?'

'No. No, I'm not.'

'I thought not. Well, I'm sure you know that I am. I came across the name of Moreton Frewen many years ago, in a memoir of the famous jockey, Fred Archer. My historical interest in the Turf is long-seated, I regret to say.' He waved a hand about him. 'You see around you the accumulation of a lifetime's fruitless scholarship. A fruitless scholarship, but a happy one. Archer rode a horse called Hampton in the Doncaster Stakes of 1876. Friday the 13th of September. It was almost exactly one hundred and ten years ago. Frewen bet every spare penny he had on Hampton to win, having consulted Archer first. It's hard to understand how the English aristocracy gambled and how pointless their lives had become. Frewen knew it well. He had decided that if he won he'd take up an offer to be master of the Kilkenny hounds in Ireland. If not, he'd go to the West. The horse lost by a head. Frewen never reproached Archer or even batted an eyelid; he clapped the jockey on the back for riding a good race and left. My God, I thought then – this was before Leslie or Andrews wrote their books – a man who can lose that well has to have something sublime about him, even if it's lunacy. I read everything I could about him. There's something about his story, something fated and Greek-tragic about his luck, that rivets attention. He's a symbolic figure. He's the landed gentry's last throw of the dice, an heroic loser on a world scale. You can't help being attracted to him. He's the apotheosis of all we horse-gambling men who've lost forever, and he's more than that. Allen Andrews compares him to a Harold trying to stop the Norman Conquest, like a representative figure of an old doomed order, that in his case was the English Landed Gentry, especially its younger sons, trying to survive and prosper when their base of wealth had gone and their power was spent. Frewen tried to use the world and its resources to redress the losses of Sussex and Ireland and Leicester. He failed, but only just. By a whisker and not for want of courage. Terrific courage. Frewen is an example to all we poor timid half-hearted backers of today's gee-gees. This country will never turn out Moreton Frewens any more. Never again.'

There was a silence. I wasn't quite sure what to say. He turned away as I let him past. I'd never heard him speak like that before.

'I'm getting old and garrulous,' he muttered. 'Saying things like those to a strapping, brave young shaver like you. I'm sorry. You'll want an invoice for your books?'

'Yes, please.'

I waited in silence while he wrote it out and handed it to me in return for my cheque. His glance upward was shy and embarrassed.

'Thank you, Mr Simpson,' he said. 'I promise not to lecture you next time. If you come again.'

'I'll come again. And you can lecture me for as long as you like. It was fascinating.'

'Well – thank you. If it helps you in your pursuit of whatever it is that you seek, I am glad.' His eyes watched me curiously, begging an answer, a clarification.

'I'm sure it will. And to be honest, I'm not sure what it is that I'm looking for. Whatever it is, Moreton Frewen is a clue to it.'

He lowered his eyelids. 'Thank you. I wish you well in your researches. And may better luck attend you, whatever you do, than attended Moreton Frewen all the days of his life.'

Chapter Eleven

I got to the Tate Gallery just as they were closing. She was waiting for me in the entrance hall. She nodded to two black-uniformed porters who were closing in on me and they dropped respectfully into the background. She beckoned me towards the interior of the building, where lights were beginning to go out and autumn shades were suddenly jumping across high domed walls with pillars and cool marble around them.

'I came as soon as I got your message,' I said.

'You were out when I phoned.' Her voice wasn't accusatory but her eyes needed an explanation. 'You weren't at the Bank.'

'I was buying books. For our library.'

'Our library?'

'Yes. Books on Moreton Frewen. By Moreton Frewen. More comprehensive books.'

She compressed her lips, receiving the doubly unwelcome inference that Frewen was still an important unresolved subject and that the books she'd read so far were insufficient, with that carefully-revealed tolerance of men's clumsiness that is the hallmark of educated women.

'Follow me.' She made it a command.

I traipsed after her through the British Collection, starting with those splendid Elizabethan portraits of severe men and women in black, with white lace collars and ruffs, punctuated by the odd florid dandy or queen in red, yellow and green brocade. She turned right and headed through into the seventeenth century, then the eighteenth. Spiky chaps in breeches stared at me as they leant on their flintlocks. A couple of spotted dogs by Stubbs sneered at me.

'Where are we going?'

She didn't answer. She walked steadily ahead, carrying her satchel-handbag slung over her shoulder, the band cutting into the epaulette of her linen jacket a bit under the weight of whatever she'd got in the bag. Her ankles were very trim; I admired the rear view.

'Is it far?'

Her heels rang on the parquet. Maritime battles slid past. John Singleton Copley's *Death of Major Pierson*, that great Jersey skirmish, confronted me, its red-coated dying hero surrounded by stricken men.

'Copley was an American,' I said irrelevantly, as we flanked it and went round the back of it into the next gallery. A porter tacked out of the gloom, saw Sue, nodded respectfully and gave a curious glance in my direction. We marched on. Rows of Turners, seagreen to start with, followed by egg-yellow with red splashes, went gliding past. We were in the Duveen rooms. She stopped, pointed to a seat facing an end wall, a rather gloomy end wall, and then gestured.

'Sit there,' she said.

I sat obediently on the bench seat, quite comfortable it was, and looked at her expectantly.

'Don't look at me! Look at the paintings! What do you see?'

A huge gaffer in riding gear, wearing a top hat, peered down at me.

'Lord Ribblesdale,' I said. 'Vast, isn't it? Legs a

mile long. There's a copy in the foyer of the Cavendish Hotel, you know. He was one of Rosa Lewis's favourites. After she'd been the family cook.'

She gave an impatient snort. 'What else?'

'Three other Sargents. That one with the children and the lanterns is called "Carnation, Lily, Lily, Rose". I remember that Sargent got so fed up with it that he called it Darnation, Silly, Silly Pose. Then there's that dim child. They're not nearly as good as the ones at the Whitney. They were in much better nick – ah! I've got it. You're going to re-hang the Sargents. That's why you made me go to the exhibition in New York. I must say that the collection at the Whitney was the best congregation of Sargents I've ever seen. Is that what this is about?'

'No.'

'What, then?'

'Can't you think? Doesn't it give you the faintest clue?'

I looked back at Lord Ribblesdale. He stared impassively towards me, an impeccable English milord in his riding kit and his black top hat. My neck began to get a crick in it. John S. Sargent painted on a large scale, with a lot of energy, for this kind of work. Lord Ribblesdale is enormous – the painting of him, I mean – stretching down a fair old expanse of wall.

'No. No, it doesn't.'

She made another gesture. It was like being in a school-room. I hate that sort of thing: tests, lessons, lectures. 'Try another tack. You're an educated man, or supposed to be. You love biography. What do you think of, when you think of Sargent portraits?'

'Society. High Society. He painted lots of 'em.'

'Who, for instance?'

'Now look, Sue – wait! I've got it! The Sitwells.

121

There was an eighteenth-century painting of the Sitwell children by Copley at Renishaw. So they got Sargent to do one of the then Sitwell family, around 1900, I think. Sir George and Lady Ida with their children, Edith, Osbert and Sacheverell.'

'Well done. You are educated. Almost. In biography especially.'

It was just like school. Nine out of ten for little Timmy.

'What else?'

'What else? Is this what you got me here for? I don't know what else. Well, what I do remember is that the painting is totally unreal. Sir George is in riding kit, which he never wore. Lady Ida is arranging flowers, which she never did, in elaborate clothes, which no lady would have worn for horticultural activities. Sir George pointed out that Edith's nose was crooked, so Sargent, who was a kindly man, painted Edith's nose straight and Sir George's crooked. I don't know what else. Give us a break, Sue. What is all this about? Was it something I was supposed to see at the Whitney?'

She stood before me, a slender but full-bosomed siren with dark brown hair and blue eyes that fixed on mine with an intensity that I didn't like the look of.

'Sargent always painted in his Tite Street studio. His clients had to go there to be painted.'

'So?'

'So in order to be painted, the Sitwells came down from Derbyshire to London to stay. They rented a house for this purpose. Osbert describes it in *Left Hand, Right Hand*. The décor was mauve and it was full of pictures of Winston Churchill.'

'Eh?'

'Winston Churchill. The address was 25 Chesham Place. It got destroyed by bombs in the 1940s, but at the time it was the house of Mr and Mrs Moreton Frewen.'

'What?'

'Clara Frewen and Jennie – Lady Randolph Churchill – made mauve a fashionable colour.'

'Hang on. I'm not following this.'

'The Frewens rented the house out because they were hard up once again. They rented it to the Sitwells. For the time of the painting of the Sargent portrait.'

'Yes, but what –'

She came up to me and stood over me so that I had to peer up the charming elevation of her to look at her face.

'Keep with the Sargent for safety,' she said. 'Not sergeant. Sargent.'

'*What?*'

'Written on those gold shares. You never saw them. Nor did Andy Casey. You got the details over the phone. You *assumed* that the spelling was that way. Actually there are forty-seven varieties, from a spelling point of view, of the very ancient surname of Sargent. It was an old English family. Frewen was notoriously ungrammatical. He might well have misspelt it.'

'Oh no. No. This is absurd.'

She reached into the satchel-handbag and pulled out a large, solid copy of *Country Life* magazine. The Autumn Gardens Number, it was. 'It hit me when I was reading this. Look!' She held it open at one of the advertising pages and stuck it under my nose. I scowled at a long picture of a pretty woman in an expensive white dress. *Mrs Cecil Wade* it said, painted in 1886 in London by John Singer Sargent. Sold at Sotheby's, New York, on Thursday 29th May for $1,485,000 (£951,923).

'Nearly a million pounds,' she said. 'And the Sargent exhibition is on, right now, at the Whitney.'

I licked my lips. My mouth had gone dry. 'This is fantastic. Far-fetched. Ridiculous.'

She stamped her foot in fury. 'Sargent!' she practically screamed at me. '*Keep with the Sargent for safety!* Don't you see? Those gold shares and other valuables must have been kept somewhere with a painting that the Frewens owned. A painting by Sargent. It wasn't a police sergeant. Or a security company. Someone is after any clue they can get, on the gold shares, or from you. You particularly.'

'This is crazy.'

'You said,' her voice dropped a bit, but it was still vibrantly urgent, 'you said that those old shares are worthless now. Absolutely worthless. Why would anyone murder for them? Why?'

'We don't know. Well, it was – damn it, you've got me confused. It was a random break-in.'

'Oh yeah? Like our flat last night? And the grab on your bags at O'Hare? Tell me, Tim, what are you well-known for?'

'Me? Me? Nothing.'

'Don't be bashful. This is no time. Who found the Gwen John sculpture? The Whistler? The Norman Shaw? What are you to someone with an inkling of the existence of a painting worth a fortune?' She grabbed my hand. 'You are the competition! White's Art Fund. You are probably well on the track of the thing. Any information you've got is relevant.'

'But I haven't got any.'

'They don't know that. They think you're hot on the trail.'

I gaped over her shoulder at Lord Ribblesdale. His face hadn't moved. One and a half million dollars. I held the edge of my seat with my spare hand.

'This won't do. This is fantasy. It's because you work at the Tate.'

'Pah!'

'The Frewens couldn't afford a Sargent. They were always broke.'

Her face changed in triumph. 'Read your books; read them carefully. There are different definitions of broke. In 1904 Clara Frewen commissioned a cast of a sculpture by Saint Gaudens at a cost of £1800 for their house, Brede Place, in Sussex. Sculpture ran in the family. Their daughter, Clare Sheridan, became a famous one. Saint Gaudens was an American. He was a friend of – guess who? Sargent. American sculpture and American painting. Why not? You could commission a Sargent for £2000 then.'

'My God! Stop this. If there were such a painting it would be well documented. Is there any mention of one? Of the Frewens?'

Her face clouded. 'No, there isn't. At least, I haven't found one so far. Not all Sargent's portraits can be accounted for, though. Oh, I know what you're going to ask, and yes, I have. At least I've started. I've been working on it all day. I've been through Stanley Olson's recent book, but that's not a *catalogue raisonnée*. There's no mention of any painting of the Frewens by Sargent in that. But you know, Tim, you know better than anyone. Work leaks out of an artist's studio all the time. Not everyone wants a record kept. Not everyone. For all sorts of reasons.'

'It's a wonderful theory, Sue. I just can't grasp it.'

My voice seemed to echo in the empty gallery. Lord Ribblesdale regarded me solemnly, with perhaps a hint of mockery. 'I realize that a Sargent is possibly very valuable nowadays. From fairly recent times only, mark you; *Mrs Cecil Wade* was a world record for a Sargent. I agree that he does fulfil so many of the requirements of the New York market. He was American, but born in Florence. He was successful in Paris and London. He was celebrated in America. You've still got to be bloody fanatical to murder for one of his works. I mean a painting can be traced.'

'Not if no one has ever seen it before. And you'd be fanatical, if it were an exceptional painting, even for a Sargent.'

'Exceptional? What do you mean?'

She stared down at me. Her face had gone pale with excitement. 'It's only a theory I've got. Something that occurred to me while looking at Carter Ratcliff's book on Sargent paintings. The one that you brought from New York.'

'What?' I was still held by the hand, tightly now. She looked fearful but very excited, a sort of feverish look that I didn't like at all.

'Sargent painted some famous threesomes, of women. The best known is the Wyndham sisters: Lady Elcho, of the Souls, Mrs Adeane and Mrs Tennant. But there were others. The Acheson sisters, the Vickers, Mrs Carl Meyer and her children, the four Boits, I don't know, probably others.'

I drew in my breath. 'You're thinking of the Jeromes?'

'Yes, Tim. Think of it! Think of a painting of those three sisters: Clara, the eldest, married to Moreton Frewen. Jennie, the middle one, married to Lord Randolph Churchill. Leonie, the youngest, married to Sir John Leslie of County Monaghan. Three famous beauties, daughters of the fabulous Leonard Jerome of New York. They took London society by storm at one time or another. Their connections are endless. What do you think the New York market would pay for a Sargent of them? All three together?'

I licked my lips again. 'A lot. A hell of a lot.'

'Exactly. And if such a painting does exist, and I feel sure it does, Tim, and if the Frewens had it or looked after it, you have been going around asking questions, as Tim Simpson of White's Art Fund, that must have set off the whole deadly business. And you acting all innocent.' She looked down at her hand, still tightly holding mine. 'The joke is that if there's one man who's most likely to find it, that man is you. So I'm not dropping out of this one. No matter what happens.'

Chapter Twelve

Jeremy White did a sort of two-step up and down his office. His face was congested. I've never seen him so agitated.

'Fantastic! Absolutely fantastic!'

'I know. It does seem far-fetched.'

'We have to find that painting!'

'What?'

He paused in his cumbersome effort at a hop, skip and jump. 'We can't risk missing it! The Art Fund must have it. It'll be the art scoop of the decade. Of the twentieth century.'

'You believe in it?'

'Of course I do. It makes absolute sense. Sargent must have painted Jennie at some time. Why not all three sisters? I've seen the Wyndhams one. The Souls! Damn it, Tim, I'm an Oxford man!'

'We've found no record of a Jerome painting to date. Not even a Jennie portrait.'

'Bah! It'll come to light. Tim, dear boy, you must get it. Forget everything else. It's your métier. This could be your finest hour. To coin a phrase. From their own family.'

'What? You, of all people! After all you've – '

'Yes, yes, I know! I know, but this is different.'

'How?'

He grabbed my arm. I'd never seen him like that before. He was like a terrier confronted by a barn full of rats. 'My dear Tim! Give me a guess – just a guess – at the value of such a painting? Bearing in mind that *Mrs Cecil Wade* fetched a million sterling. Guess?'

I sighed. I'd thought about that. 'Two million sterling? Three million dollars? In New York, of course.'

'At least! At least! I can think of five American museums who'd pay that. It's not only a superb portrait by an Anglo-American master. It's a social document. The Jeromes came from upstate New York. It's a –'

'Steady on, Jeremy. You're going to burst a blood vessel in a minute. Superb painting? You haven't even seen it yet. If it exists.'

'It exists! I know it exists! I feel it in my bones. It must exist. I believe in it.'

'That's what frightens me. You and Sue both jumped at the idea.'

He stopped his agitated movement. 'What do you mean?'

'It's so believable. Something a real forger could pass off so well. Sargent is a very paintable painter. There are plenty of photos of the sisters to use as models. A forgery like that would be well worth it.'

'My dear Tim! You are so devious, sometimes.'

'It wouldn't be the first occasion some clever criminal has laid a trail for Simpson to follow. Start me off with Frewen and lead me on to something exciting like this. You see, it's all such clever psychology. People who've bought forgeries, obvious forgeries like those Palmers of Keating's, have done so because they wanted those forgeries to exist. They wanted to believe in them, despite all evidence to the contrary, because the forgery fulfilled some romantic or material need. This is a bit like that.'

'Good heavens. You are a cool customer these days.

The Art Fund is well guarded.' He smiled crookedly. 'We can muster experts for authentication, surely?'

'Indeed we can. Which makes us all the more dangerous to a forger. You've carefully avoided talking about danger, so far. This has become a game for very high stakes, Jeremy. You're sure you want to play, are you? I'm game, of course, but let's have no moaning at the bar if things go wrong.'

'Hm.' He stroked his jaw. 'Forgeries and danger. I don't want to expose you or Sue to danger. Which means that the sooner we resolve this the better. We have to get an idea where to start. Chicago is the obvious place.'

'Why?'

'The gold-mine documents. You said they turned up there in the 'twenties. Originally they were kept with the Sargent. It might be there too. Frewen could have sold the lot when he was out of funds.'

'It doesn't fit. A painting like that would have been recorded. He sold his mother-in-law's diamond necklace to finance his gold-crusher; that's in every book about him; don't think he wouldn't have told everyone if he'd sold the family painting too. Everyone has heard about the Holbein that was in the family home, Brickwall in Sussex. Moreton used to bounce a ball against it when he was a boy, but it's in the Metropolitan, or the Frick, now. That's famous. A Sargent would be, too.'

'You don't know.' His agitation was coming back. 'Don't be so negative. We must check every possibility – wait! I've got it! Get your coat!'

'What?'

'Donald. We never even started to tap Donald. We said we'd talk to him again. Come on, we'll take my car. He'll be delighted to see us. Donald is the fount of all knowledge on the Frewens, and he's a member of the family. There's no time to lose. The quicker this thing is ended, the quicker the danger will go.'

'What about the Bank? Today's work?'

'To hell with the Bank! Get your coat.'

Nothing would have it but that we had to rush down into the garage basement beneath the Bank immediately and roar off into the City of London in Jeremy's saloon Jaguar, him cursing at the traffic all the way to the suburbs. Once we got out on to the Portsmouth Road he calmed down a bit, enough to keep the speed at ninety miles an hour anyway, and to stop swearing. We drove through lunch-time and, the way Jeremy handled the car, the Devil's Punchbowl and Hindhead came up like landing lights on an aircraft runway. In no time at all we had turned off the road, bounced in a cloud of dust past the supercilious stallion and skidded to a halt at the front door, spraying gravel everywhere.

Donald White gaped at us in amusement as he opened the front door. 'Jeremy? Tim? What's this? Playing truant?'

'Want to talk to you.' Jeremy was brisk.

'Me? A retired old codger? I am honoured. What's up at the Bank? Business a bit slack?'

'No, no. Need your advice. Your memory. Can we come in?'

'Of course you can.' Donald held the door open. 'Have you had lunch? Can I get you something?'

'A coffee would be great,' I managed to get in before Jeremy refused any refreshment. 'Jeremy's short-circuited our lunch today.'

'In that case I'll do the honours.' He turned and beckoned us to follow him, limping his way ahead.

I didn't remember the house. I hadn't been inside

before. The garden party had been literally that; with such good weather that Sunday, now seemingly distant, we had all stayed outside. The interior was a pleasant surprise, oak-beamed, tile-floored, smelling of polish. Good rugs, Kazaks, and Turkomans, lay on the tiles. We followed him through a hall, a sitting-room with an inglenook fireplace, a dining-room with an oak refectory table and a dresser I vaguely recognized, into a kitchen. It was small, compact, neatly-stowed. We had to stay behind a bar-counter while Donald went into a central area surrounded by the working instruments of the kitchen.

'Just like a ship's galley,' he explained. 'Crock like me can't do with others inside the working area. Everything to hand for one cook. Broth won't get spoiled that way. Here, have some cheese while I brew up your coffee.'

He wore a dark blue sweater and canvas trousers. His brown face regarded us shrewdly, and his expression, senior and experienced, made Jeremy remember his manners and keep his impetuous questions in check, to be held back until Donald indicated he was ready. When he had served us coffee and we were sitting at the kitchen counter, sipping from mugs and consuming fresh bread and cheese, Donald sat himself down on a stool opposite us and gave us both a keen stare.

'Now then,' he demanded, 'what's all this about?'

Jeremy cleared his throat. He'd restrained himself with great difficulty. 'It's your knowledge of Frewen we want to tap,' he began.

'Oh no! I thought you wanted my help as a banker. How disappointing. I thought I was going to be brought out of retirement.' Donald's voice was mocking but his eyes didn't twinkle. I sensed that his disappointment had more than a touch of reality to it.

'Well – sorry – you did say we could come back to you about Frewen.'

'Of course I did. Pay no attention to my howl of frustration. What about him this time?'

'Donald, did your father ever mention him in connection with a painting? By Sargent?'

Donald's head came up and his eyes widened. He put down his own coffee mug. 'Sargent? You mean John Singer Sargent?'

'Yes.'

'Good grief.' Donald seemed quite taken aback. 'A painting? What sort of painting?'

'We assume it was a portrait. Of him and/or his wife. Or – ' Jeremy warmed to his enthusiasm before I had time to check him, to let any suggestion come from Donald himself and not to put ideas into his head – 'of the three sisters, the Jerome sisters? Sargent painted several famous threesomes.'

'Good God!' Donald's eyes opened even wider and his mouth dropped. 'You mean Jennie Jerome? Lady Randolph Churchill? With Clara Frewen? And that other sister, the younger one, she married an Irishman, I've forgotten her name.'

'Leonie.'

'That's it. Leonie. Good grief. No, I can't say I have. How on earth has this idea come about?'

I explained to him very briefly how the whole thing had arisen. He listened in mounting incredulity. 'But I say! This is very tenuous, isn't it? I mean, good heavens, it must be possible, surely, to substantiate whether Sargent painted the three ladies or not?'

'Not so far. Well, to be honest, the evidence so far is contrary.'

'There you are! I mean, the idea of the writing being spelt the wrong way – though hang on a minute!

Moreton Frewen was notoriously ungrammatical. He was a friend of Kipling's, but that didn't stop him from mucking up the punctuation of Winston's first book when he sent it to Frewen from India. Frewen got it published, but Winston was quite upset, because he said that after Uncle Moreton had checked through it, everyone thought it had been mangled by a mad proof-reader. I suppose it is possible that he meant a Sargent not a sergeant. But my God, it's hardly evidence, is it?'

Jeremy made an impatient gesture. 'Maybe not. But it's a possibility. Worth following up. Following up actively.'

Donald gave him an amused glance. 'You are becoming a fanatic, Jeremy. I can see that you and Tim put your Art Fund in front of everything.'

'No!' Jeremy stood up. He hates thinking in a seated position. Stretching himself to his full height, he stepped back from the counter. 'It's not that. Not that at all. I've got something here – ' he tapped the side of his head – 'something nagging me. Something about Sargent. Something at the back of my mind. I can't put my finger on it, it won't come out, but it's something important. God, I wish I had the time to look into it properly.'

Donald gave me a meaning stare and a faint wink. 'You're quite obsessive, my dear chap. What sort of thing?'

'I don't know. Something someone told me years ago.'

'But come on!' Donald voiced an opinion I'd already given several times. 'If such an important painting was executed, it was commissioned by somebody, painted by Sargent, and paid for by that somebody. It didn't just materialize out of thin air. Sargent was a prolific and energetic painter. I accept that there must be a lot of his work still uncatalogued, but not something like this, this threesome of Jeromes. My God, every art foundation in America would be after a thing like that.'

'Exactly! Exactly!'

Donald shook his head. 'I've never heard of such a thing.'

'Your father never spoke of it?'

He grinned. 'My father only spoke of money lost on mad schemes like gold-crushers and tramways and opening up Kenya or Australia. Frewen had a fortune in his hands at Broken Hill and then let them cheat him of it. There were far greater dramas to talk about than oil paintings, let me tell you. Everyone was being painted by Sargent before the First War. It was no subject of conversation.'

'Damn it.' Jeremy was crestfallen. 'I felt sure you'd have some sort of lead for us.'

'Sorry, Jeremy. No can do.'

We finished our snack talking of Bank matters. Jeremy seemed to pull himself together and, realizing that Donald had been a bit disappointed at our avoidance of Bank consultation with him, made a real effort to brief him on current Bank affairs and to ask his opinion. It pleased me to see that side of Jeremy in action; he can be very considerate that way. After about half an hour he heaved himself up and announced that we must go, thanking Donald profusely.

'Oh, don't thank me. I'm sorry I've been of such little help.'

'Of course you've been of help. It's been jolly useful, hasn't it, Tim?'

'It certainly has.'

Jeremy looked about him. 'You've got a new dresser.'

Donald grinned. 'I wondered if you'd notice. Bought it at the rooms. Not yours, your competitors'. Always needed a good oak dresser in here.'

'It's very handsome.'

It was a large pot-board dresser of the early eighteenth century, with a frilly rack of shelves above. I realized that it was the one that had given me a faint pang of recognition but that it was a classic of its type, worth about three thousand pounds.

'What do you think, Tim?'

'Very fine. Fits in here perfectly.'

'Ah. Glad you like it.' Donald smiled at me. 'I turfed out a mahogany sideboard that didn't suit the house at all and it more than paid for this one.'

'Well, that's fashion for you. Mahogany is in, right now, but oak is out. The fashion for it, anyway.'

'It'll change, I suppose?'

'Oh yes. These things always do.'

He limped with us to the car, slapped the roof in a farewell gesture and moved across the gravel towards his horse. Jeremy drove out of the gates and turned towards London, biting his lip.

'What a waste of time,' he growled. 'There's something I simply can't place, Tim.'

'It's not Donald's fault. You have to consider that the painting might not exist.'

'Oh, Tim, really! You are the most negative man, sometimes. I – '

The phone rang, surprising him. Jeremy installed a car phone some time ago. He thought it would befit his senior and important executive role. I happen to know that he leaves it out of the car frequently, especially at weekends, because in his heart of hearts he hates the thing. There really have to be occasions when a man isn't available, and driving the car is arguably one of them. An expression of annoyance came out of him.

'Really! I did give instructions that I wasn't to be contacted on that infernal thing unless it was really urgent.'

'This might be.'

'Nonsense.' He wrenched the receiver off its fitting and put it to his ear. 'Hello? Now look here – who? Oh. From Chicago? Great heavens. And here we are in the car. You're patching the call through? How?'

'The miracles of modern technology,' I said.

He snorted and passed the instrument over. 'It's for you.'

'Me? Good grief. No escape for the wicked. Hello?'

The line was crackly but the voice was clear, quite undeniably clear and distinct so that, afterwards, there was no doubt as to what had been said. 'Tim? Hi, this is Andy. Andy Casey. I told you I wouldn't let this thing drop. I persuaded Maguire to carry out another house-to-house round Victor Perkins's street near the Sunset Valley golf course. It's a quiet, modest residential area. Four people picked out a photograph of Kamrowski as being one of three guys they'd seen hanging round the area before the murder. They held an ID parade yesterday. They were positive. All of them. Kamrowski was one of the people staking out Perkins's place before they broke in. Are you listening?'

'Yes, I am.' My mind raced and my hand shook a bit, but that might have been the car. 'The thing is that Kamrowski was the bag snatcher at the airport.'

'Exactly. There is a direct connection between the two events. You were a precisely-located target. It

137

was not a random snatch, any more than our break-in was. You were a target. You most probably still are.' His voice was triumphant. 'I thought you ought to know that. As soon as possible.'

Chapter Thirteen

'In principle,' I said, closing the report, 'the branch in Chicago is a high-risk venture. What we have done is to spell out how costly it is likely to be if it fails totally. In other words, if it attracted no new business at all. The other estimates are purely subjective. How much business do you think you will attract; how much you'll take from competitors; how long it will take; and so on. These are pure speculation, if you like, but speculation with an element of calculation in it. It quantifies the elements of timing and cost.'

I was beginning to sound like an accountant. Charles Massenaux gave me one of his secret smiles, half encouraging, half sardonic. Howarth rustled his papers at the other end of the table. Carlton sat on his right. The other directors sat or lounged in attitudes of keen alertness or laconic indifference as suited their individual styles. We were in the conference room over Christerby's in London, the room that is used for board meetings. Beneath and around us, the bustle of business could be heard; porters were moving chunks of continental furniture into the largest of the auction rooms for a sale the following week.

'You haven't said – ' one of the alert directors with a rather plaintive voice spoke to me – 'how much business *you* think we'd get if this, this very expensive venture, I may say, were to be undertaken?'

'No, I haven't. Because I don't know. I am not an executive director of this company. It is for them and

139

their managers to provide such estimates, and they have. Those estimates are included in the various projections in my report.'

'Hmph.' He didn't say it, but the inference was clear; Simpson was avoiding the issue. It wasn't a fair inference, of course, and I did have my own idea of what was realistic by way of achievement, but I wasn't going to commit myself at this meeting, in front of this lot. It was for Howarth and Carlton to do that, not me.

'On the other hand – ' by speaking I brought the plaintive one's head up again, to look at me – 'on the other hand, when you consider that we have regional branches in Britain – Edinburgh, Chester, Bristol and Worthing – a relatively small country of sixty-odd million people, it does not seem a conflicting principle to apply the same reasoning to the United States, a richer country of nearly, what, two hundred and forty million, with a much wider geographical spread.'

'Ah, quite. But you ignore the element of competition.'

'Not in my report I don't.'

'We're not without competition in Britain.' Howarth's voice cut in from the top of the table. 'We're keeping our place in the big four only because we are as efficient, as expert, and as well known as the other three. We're not frightened of taking on competition. The fact is that a business like ours either has to become a major force in the USA or expect, eventually, to become a branch of a big American auctioneer. The historical progression is inevitable.' He paused for a moment to let the contentious statement, with its wider cultural and psychological implications, sink in. Then he continued. 'What I'm sure we're all grateful to Tim for is doing an excellent job of work in setting out the facts and figures involved. We can all be quite clear in our minds just what, from now on, it is we're taking on.'

The phrase 'job of work' was so like the man. It brought to mind a smithy full of blacksmiths hammering out bolts of iron for a black boiler factory. I made a fractional bow in his direction as a response to his tribute. Charles Massenaux gave me another slightly mocking quirk of his lips and a meaningful glance, as though there were some deep, political significance or implication to which only he and I were party. I knew what the decision would mean to Charles; the radical alteration of the focus of the business, a powerful pull westward, the elevation of Carlton to a much, much more powerful position, providing that Howarth overcame the reservations he'd voiced to me in New York during my visit.

'Can we hear Mr Carlton on the subject?' The plaintive one's voice piped up bravely. 'I'm sure we all endorse Harry Howarth's feelings on the usefulness of Tim Simpson's figures but – ' damning with faint praise – 'it will, after all, fall to Mr Carlton and his team to, er, to execute this possible project and it is he, as the man on the spot, to whom we must all look for some sort of guidance, no, not guidance, er, commitment, perhaps?'

Aha, thinks Simpson at this point, he's getting you to stick your neck out, Alex, sliding the block beneath it so that, at some time in the future, if all goes awry you can take the chopper where it normally hits the turkey just before Christmas. Or Thanksgiving, in your case.

Carlton wasn't an American for nothing. He looked straight at the plaintive one through his gold-rimmed spectacles, which made his eyes look somehow barer and more intense than heavier frames might have done.

'I'm confident we can succeed,' he said in a flat, unemotional tone. 'We have the right people, we have the right backing, and our reputation in the States is growing every day. Tim's estimates are, necessarily, conservative. I believe we can achieve his first budget for break-even in two years and perhaps exceed it. Chicago and the mid-West is a relatively undeveloped area in our line of business. My people are keen to tackle it. We must go ahead.'

Howarth gave him a look that combined extreme satisfaction with what I detected to be an element of slight surprise. It was as though Carlton's commitment was much more positive than he'd been expecting. Howarth looked boldly down the long table.

'Good,' he said crisply, taking his cue at that moment and, sensibly, not waiting a minute more for anyone to shove an oar in. 'I move that we vote, then. The proposal is – '

And that was it. The board rallied to the flag. Considering it was a special meeting, that it was Friday afternoon going on six o'clock, and that we'd missed our Café Royal lunch, they behaved very well. I had a suspicion that some of them were disinclined to argue on the grounds that it might delay the start of their weekend, so that they all voted in favour. Howarth was as pleased as a dog with two whatsits, having got himself a unanimous board decision. He came up to me as they were clearing off and I was scraping up my papers, and clapped me on the back.

'Well done, Tim! Thanks for everything.'

'My congratulations to you. It's all gone very well for you and Alex.'

'It has indeed. I hope we won't have any ructions from Jeremy?'

'Oh, Jeremy'll be all right. For the moment.' I gave him a significant smile. 'It'll be in a year or so's time that you might have trouble with Jeremy.'

'No, we won't. We'll be very successful, you'll see.'

'I'm sure you will. Particularly with Alex so committed to it.'

'Indeed. He was very positive, wasn't he?'

'Very impressive. They couldn't say no after that – ah, here he is. Hi, Alex. My congratulations. You're all set for the Windy City.'

'Thank you.' He gave me a broad smile. 'It will be a challenging time for us. I do hope your role won't end here? We'll be seeing you again in New York? And Chicago?'

'Oh, I expect so. You don't get rid of me that easily. I have to coordinate finance with Andy Casey and all that. There's plenty to do.'

'Good.' He gave me a long stare before turning to Howarth. 'What time do we have to leave, Harry?'

'Right now.' The other looked at his watch. 'Right now. There's a train from Paddington very soon.' He turned to me. 'Alex is staying on a day or so to go over things before he heads back to the States.'

'Good idea. I hope you have a nice weekend. See you both again soon, I'm sure.'

'Thanks, Tim. All the best.'

'Me too.'

I turned to find Charles Massenaux standing beside me. 'I suppose,' he queried, with a tinge of the playful sarcasm that often colours his remarks to me, 'that you won't have time for a drink with a mere

British company director? I mean, I realize that your thoughts are purely transatlantic now, but – '

'Enough, Charles! Enough. Of course I'll have a drink with you. Providing you are paying, of course.'

Chapter Fourteen

Although it was Saturday morning, Mr Goodston's shop was deserted. He sat immobile behind his desk, his face concealed by a leather-bound volume. At the tinkle of the bell, his eyes came up over the top of the book and his half-moons widened at the sight of me.

'Mr Simpson!' The tone was of quiet surprise. 'Back already? This fine Saturday morning? I had imagined you to be somewhere out in the air, the field perhaps, water, or the moor? Not frowsting here in London, in my poor, dusty shop of all places.'

' 'Morning, Mr Goodston. I wished to consult you. Therefore I am here.'

'Consult me?' He put down the book, prised the wire frame of his glasses off his nose and peered at me before brushing vaguely at the rumpled waistcoat that contained the bulging, inchoate mass of his torso. 'Consult me? I am a poor bookseller, my dear sir, but my advice is available if you seek it. Provided – ' he held up an admonitory finger – 'you are not here to ask for a tip on the gee-gees. I have made it a rule, indeed a principle, never to give advice on matters of the Turf. One makes enemies that way.'

I smiled at him. He was so perfectly suited to his environment, to the dusty ranks of literature on the ancient wood shelves, to the grime-filtered light of his plate-glass window. It was a world removed from reality, a world of concept and memoir, of record and frozen image, long captured and petrified into numb, desensitized history.

'No tips for the races. I quite agree with you; such advice must be a hazard.'

He moistened his lips. 'Have you read the books you bought from me?'

'I have, thank you.'

'Did they provide the clue you were seeking?'

'No. I'm afraid they didn't.'

'Ah.' A cautionary look appeared on his face, as though he suspected that I might try to return them, but he suppressed the expression.. 'I'm sorry. Is that the matter on which you have come to consult me?'

'In a way.'

'But not directly?'

I compressed my lips. 'The book by Allen Andrews was – is – excellent. I agree with you and with Ralph Martin, whose book on Lady Randolph Churchill I have now read, in its two volumes. He says exactly what you say in his chapter notes. Andrews's book is more comprehensive, more factual, less involved than Anita Leslie's. On the other hand, Anita Leslie's is very readable and there are reminiscences of hers that add to the book by Andrews. In a way, the two are complementary. Anita Leslie doesn't really try to explain Moreton Frewen's vast, intricate and disastrous financial dealings. Andrews does so at length; it explains how Frewen's whole life, and tragically that of his wife and children, was poisoned by debts, legal action, entails, mortgages, bailiffs – it's like something out of Dickens.'

'Very true.' Mr Goodston sighed. 'Once the initial loss passes beyond a certain point, everything that follows is lost capital, sunk investment. In trying to recoup that vast initial loss, the judgment becomes impaired and the situation simply gets worse. It's a principle of gambling, you know.' His face sagged in knowledge.

'By initial loss, you're referring in this case to Wyoming?'

'Precisely. That crash haunted Frewen for the rest of his life. It wrecked his judgment. From then on he snatched at opportunities which were, many of them, premature.'

I stuck my hands in my pockets. 'In a way you can blame his brother Richard for Wyoming. If Richard hadn't insisted on pulling out, Moreton wouldn't have had to pay off his share. To do that he had to form a public company and raise capital over here, thus locking himself in. He lost his independence.'

Mr Goodston rolled his eyes. 'If Richard hadn't pulled out, Moreton would just have lost all their money instead of their money and that of all the other investors.'

'You're hard, Mr Goodston. But probably right. If he had inherited the estate of Moreton Old Hall in Cheshire from his godfather, as he should have, he'd probably have lost that too. Frewen's life is full of ifs.'

'Indeed. What did you think of his own book, *Melton Mowbray*?'

'I enjoyed it, even if the style is quixotically old-fashioned, and the memoirs remarkable for what they don't say rather than for what they do. He really must be unique in having had a personal one-man guided tour of the site of the Little Big Horn battle by Sitting Bull himself; to have had that sort of experience is incredible. I loved some of the horsey stories too. The other side of the coin is that it makes one so grateful for modern biography. In Frewen's day, public utterance and reminiscence had to be too circumspect, too cautious. Then there was that preoccupation with style. It's like Osbert Sitwell's memoirs, really; they only come to life, for me, when his father appears on the scene and Osbert is so upset and enraged by the thought of the old, eccentric devil that he forgets to use those long, convoluted clauses.'

'But the clue you were seeking: *Melton Mowbray* didn't provide it?'

'I'm afraid not. That's why I've come to see you.'

'Would you like to sit down?' He waved at a rather decrepit chair, birch-framed, but with frayed caning to the seat, that leant rather than stood against a bookcase near his paper-clogged desk. I sat down on it and opened my mouth, but he held up his hand.

'A moment. Do you, by any chance, drink sherry?'

'Of course.'

'In that case, may I offer you a glass? If you will forgive my observation, your face contains within it the traces of a serious preoccupation. Perhaps if we sip a glass of sherry while we talk, it may help to – to resolve the matter?'

'That's very kind. I'd love a sherry.'

He smiled broadly. 'Your acceptance gives me the justification for an indulgence which I regret occasions guilt within me.' He heaved himself to his feet. 'The law of England upon the hours of drinking in public houses has corrupted the independence of the nation's mind on its own habits. Before the First War, no one would have imagined that the population could be told when it could drink.'

'I quite agree. A Frenchman finds it absurd.'

'True.' He shuffled behind a sagging bookcase to a cabinet, out of my sight, and returned with a bottle of Celebration Cream and two large tulip glasses. A surprisingly clean white cloth emerged from the top drawer of his overloaded desk and he polished the two glasses with it carefully, holding each up to the light before placing them on a small clear area among the heaps of books on the desk's top surface. Then, with great precaution, he poured the sherry into the glasses, decanting perhaps a sixth of the bottle into each one. I made no comment on the quantity he had provided but held up my glass in a silent toast before I drank.

'Excellent,' I said. 'Just the ticket.'

He smiled again, slumping himself back into his desk chair like a collapsing bag of rumpled tweed cloth and individual checked waistcoat that insulated him from the air of the bookshop, cooler this morning due to a fresh breeze rustling down Praed Street on its way to Paddington Station.

'Tell me,' I said, working my way round to an idea that had occurred to me in the dark hours of the night, when with wide-open eyes I had listened to Sue's erratic breathing beside me, telling me Sue was having a bad night too, 'how much of the real nature of late Victorian and Edwardian high society has ever really been revealed to us?'

He put down his sherry glass which, I noticed, was already half empty. 'A large question,' he said. 'Rather too large a question, I think. Could you not perhaps be a little more, er, a little more specific? Which aspect do you have in mind? I mean – ' he waved an arm grandiloquently at the millions of words which surrounded him – 'sporting, military and thespian specialities. These you see are merely the tip of an iceberg. They recount, with varying degrees of veracity, spite, objectivity, truthfulness and down-right lies, one part of one aspect of the doings of various people. The real truth, if there is such a thing, will never be known to us. Almost certainly never.'

'Indeed. I was thinking of something connected with the relationships within that society. The ruling part of society. It was quite a small number of people, really, who held all the power. I think Churchill said 20,000, or something like that.'

'Relationships?'

'Er, I meant sexual relationships. Between men and women. Very often married men and married women.'

'Ah.' Comprehension filtered into his features. '"Never comment on a likeness" perhaps, do you mean?'

'Exactly. If some of the literature is to be believed, London and country house society involved a great deal of, er, mixed bathing.'

'The Marlborough House Set, for instance?'

'Yes. And the hunting crowd. There was much tacit understanding, discreet bedroom arrangements. Provided no scandal ever ensued, everyone was quite reconciled to all their sort of –'

'Hypocrisy?'

'Well, we think of it as hypocrisy now, perhaps, but it was their accommodation with human nature.'

'There was – and is – much exaggeration, I believe. If many accounts are to be credited, the practice of calling on ladies at tea-time involved the most fevered adulteries, whereas –'

'Whereas, in fact, as Anita Leslie points out, the presence of servants and the cocooning nature of the clothes the ladies wore would have made the reality of the granting of favours very difficult.'

'You put it well, my dear sir. You put it well. I have no doubt that, as always, there were – what did they call it? – ardent, yes, ardent ones, who would behave promiscuously, as in any age. But there was, then, a great deal more truly romantic love, hopelessly unrequited love, than this modern age, with its insistence on instantly-gratified appetite, would tolerate.' Mr Goodston polished off his sherry with a smack of the lips and held up the bottle with a querying expression in my direction.

'Just a suspicion, thank you. I still have some.'

He topped up my glass and replenished his own. 'People then, men of wealth particularly, seemed quite content to worship married ladies, ply them with flowers and presents, in return for what was, quite often, friendly companionship. The men hoped, perhaps they hoped, but in a way, had their secret fantasy been granted, it would have destroyed the illusion, shattered the pure love. There's a story of Somerset Maugham's along those lines.' He glanced at his shelves. 'I include him for his theatrical connections.'

'Words can be difficult. The euphemisms they used. I mean "The King dined with Mrs X. last night." What did they mean? Sometimes it was clear, sometimes not. "The King dined with Lady Dudley," they said, the night – '

'The night Persimmon won the Derby! Ha!' Mr Goodston called it out excitedly, as though he'd been there himself. 'I think you can be sure of what the word "dined" meant that night! His horse had won the Derby and he savoured his triumph to the full. And yet, and yet; Lady Randolph twitted him for having been "jilted" by Lady Dudley. That was, perhaps, later. Or out of jealousy.'

'So you see, it's difficult to know.'

'Indeed.' He stared expectantly at me.

'Mr Goodston, I am trying to find a painting by Sargent. John Singer Sargent. It is possible that it is of the Frewens. It is also possible, perhaps more probable, that it is of the three Jerome sisters. At some point in their lives. I haven't found it yet, so I don't know.'

Mr Goodston made a bubbling noise. For a moment I thought that sherry was going to spout from him, perhaps from his ears. He choked at me for several seconds, going redder in the face and swelling like a frog in ecstasy.

'Are you OK? Shall I give you a tap on the back?'

He shook his head. An eructation shook him and the convexity deflated. He coughed, loudly. 'A Sargent! Of the Jerome sisters? My dear fellow! Such a painting would be extremely valuable.'

'It would.'

'I mean, think of his famous rendition of the Wyndham sisters. Astounding. God knows what that would fetch now.'

'I'm afraid it's not much use thinking. The Wyndham sisters are in the Metropolitan, in New York. Paintings as important as that don't come on the market. Not very often, anyway.'

'Who commissioned this canvas you seek? Leonard Jerome?'

I sighed. 'I'm afraid its existence is a speculation. We can find no evidence of it.'

'None?'

'None. Not so far. That's why I've come to see you.'

'Me? Mr Simpson, you run an Art Fund. I am a bookseller. Surely there is an antithesis in this?'

'A paradox, rather. But not such a paradox. Your speciality is certain aspects of society which, as it happens, were very important to the period I'm dealing with. I lay awake all last night. Sue – my girlfriend from the Tate – and I can find no record of such a painting in any work on Sargent. Neither Moreton Frewen, who was not an aesthete, nor Lord Randolph Churchill, nor Sir John Leslie, the husbands of the ladies concerned, appear to have commissioned such a work. Frewen's daughter Clare was painted by Emile Fuchs, one of Sargent's rivals. But no reference to Sargent can I find. Hence my line of thinking. Could someone else, another admirer, have commissioned it? And kept it secret? Could such a thing have been possible?'

Mr Goodston regarded me with what I recognized as a little awe. A thoughtful expression deepened on his face.

'Anita Leslie says her grandmother was always instructed never to comment on a likeness.'

Mr Goodston smiled slightly, his expression still deep and his eyes fixed on mine. 'Relationships were very interwoven' he murmured, almost to himself. 'Some conversations must have been minefields for the gauche and the ingenuous.' He gestured at the bookshelves. 'The tip of the iceberg. The tip of the iceberg.'

'That's what I was thinking. About the Sargent. And who commissioned it. And paid for it.'

'Could it have been concealed?'

'Goya concealed the nude Maja from the Duchess's husband. He only saw the clothed version. Anything is possible. Sargent was a fellow American. He could be discreet.'

Mr Goodston gave me a sharp glance. 'So who is your candidate?'

'For Clara, King Milan of Serbia. For Jennie, well, Edward the Seventh himself, or Kinsky, or . . . I don't know. For Leonie, the Duke of Connaught.

Both Edward and Connaught were themselves painted by Sargent.'

'My goodness.' He took off his glasses. 'You have done your research well. Most thoroughly. I congratulate you. Those were, indeed, the principal admirers of those three ladies. Or, at least, the ones that history knows of.'

'The problem,' I said with emotion, for it had been plaguing me all night and all through all the books I had read, 'the problem is that I can find no connection between Sargent and any of the three Jerome sisters. None at all. If only there were a lead of some sort I could feel encouraged. As it is, I'm stuck.'

He frowned at me. 'I beg your pardon?'

'I'm stuck. I can't make a connection.'

His frown deepened. 'But you said you had read all the Leslie books? Your, er, friend, Sue got them for you?'

'She did. There's nothing in them.'

With a shake of his head, he put his glasses back. 'We appear to be talking at cross purposes. You've covered the Leslie-Jerome connection?'

'Yes. All Anita's books.'

'No, no! Not Anita. Seymour.'

'Seymour? Who's Seymour?'

'My dear chap!' He heaved himself to his feet. 'I am most fearfully sorry! I made an assumption. Quite wrong of me, of course. Let me enlighten you.'

He shuffled sharply over to his shelves and skittered his fingers along them. 'Ah! Here we are! *The Jerome Connection*, by Seymour Leslie. He was Anita's uncle. One of Leonie's four sons. His memoirs are here. A rich source. John Murray, 1964. Blue cloth, fine. Surely, as I remember – ah! Here we are! Page 38. Opposite. Look, my dear fellow, look!'

He held the book under my nose. A strong charcoal sketch of a handsome woman, her face starting to thicken under the chin, her eyes down, met my gaze. 'Lady Randolph Churchill in 1900, as I first remember her, by John Sargent, RA,' the caption said. I could see the signature on the print: John S. Sargent.

'Mr Goodston! Jesus! Mr Goodston! He drew her! Is there any mention of a painting?' My voice roared through the shop, but Mr Goodston, smiling, shook his head. 'The acknowledgment is to Mrs Hugo Pitman for permitting reproduction of her uncle John Sargent's charcoal drawing of Lady Randolph Churchill. No mention of any painting. I fancy they would have used it if there had been one. The book – ' his voice was mild but full of pleasure – 'is yours for £20.'

'Done! My God! Done! I'll have it. We've made it! A genuine connection! Why the *hell* isn't it mentioned anywhere else? Not even in Martin's book?'

He shook his head. 'I've no idea. Perhaps it wasn't considered important. After all, Sargent went out of fashion for many years. Portrait-painting is such a fickle business I'm sure I don't need to tell you that.'

'I have to go!' I fumbled for my wallet. 'I have to get to Jeremy! He'll hit the sky when I tell him! Sargent certainly drew Jennie. Why not the others? Why not a joint portrait?'

'You'll find – ' Mr Goodston's eyes were sparkling – 'that Seymour Leslie isn't too keen on Moreton Frewen. An unwelcome relative who only came to borrow, I seem to recollect he calls him.'

'You don't know what you've done! I'm off! Mr Goodston, you are a jewel, a scholar beyond compare!' I hurled down a £20 note. 'Thanks for the sherry! Thanks for everything!'

'Mr Simpson.' His tone made me stop just as I reached the door.

'What?' I was all afire, eager to be off.

He waved a hand at the shelves. 'The tip of the iceberg. Some of this history is very recent. Very recent. You said yourself it's difficult to know. You talked of secrets. Anything is possible, you said, and you quoted "Never comment on a likeness." Much of history that has not come to light has not come to light for very good reasons, my dear young sir. Reasons of distress and upset, reasons that dictate that some of the past is best left alone. Surely I don't have to tell you, of all people? Digging up the past can be a very dangerous business. A very dangerous business indeed. I do counsel you to take care; I should hate to lose one of my most promising younger clients.'

Chapter Fifteen

'I do wish,' said Sue crossly, as I hurled the Jaguar coupé into the first gratifying open stretch of the Kingston bypass, 'that Jeremy would not disconnect his radio telephone. Or his car telephone. It really is too bad that we have to spend the best part of our Saturday chasing about after him like this.'

'Jeremy is no fool. He wants the weekend off. Ergo, he has disconnected the phone. He will reconnect it again once he is at sea. For safety reasons. This is good news for us. It means he's still up at the jetty.'

'He's not at a jetty. His boat is on a buoy.'

Women are very contentious. Especially curators of art museums with feminist and teacher-like tendencies. They can't resist correcting you. This time, however, she was wrong.

'His boat normally rides on a buoy at the Hamble. I grant you that. It is not at the Hamble right now. It is at Chichester Harbour. That is why I am doing one hundred and ten miles an hour down the Portsmouth Road, not the M3 motorway. Oops!'

'That man shook his fist at you. How do you know that? About Chichester, I mean?'

'The children's nanny told me. On the phone. Jeremy and Mary have sneaked off for a sailing weekend. Well, they couldn't leave till lunch-time. It's one of the last fine weekends of autumn so they scarpered. Don't blame them; it'll soon be too cold for casual jaunts.'

'Why isn't the boat on the Hamble?'

'Because,' I said patiently, swerving round a car that insisted on staying in the fast lane at only eighty miles an hour, 'the whole point of sailing on the Solent is that you can put in for the night at all sorts of neat little places like Cowes and the Isle of Wight, or you can nip up the coast to Chichester and Dell Quay or Bosham and in all of them there'll be a pub and a dinner and a bit of convivial company. It's a mite tame for your ocean-going fanatic but for a nice, pleasant, safe weekend's sailing it takes a lot of beating. I expect Jeremy intends to sail back from Chichester to the Hamble so that he's in a position for the winter or something. He gets so little time for sailing at present.'

'He doesn't do too badly.' Her voice was still sharp. 'Mary gets a bit cheesed off with all that sailing sometimes.'

'But she goes with him. I realize that not many women are keen on the briny but I thought Mary was quite enthusiastic.'

She shot me a glance that said what would you know about what Mary or any other woman really thinks and what she shows by way of enthusiasms, it's all part of a vast, complex, carefully-planned manœuvring for position that only women understand.

'I still think it could have waited,' she said petulantly.

I ignored that. I'd already explained that a find as important as the charcoal sketch by Sargent of Lady Randolph Churchill meant that there might be a very good reason for spending time, money and resources in trying to locate the Sargent referred to on Frewen's share envelope, a Sargent whose existence she, indeed, had suggested. There are times when it doesn't do to over-emphasize these matters. A small affair of two million sterling doesn't stimulate your museum curator much, either, it seems; they live in a world of scholarship, you see. Nothing like ours.

'1900 seems to have been a key date,' I said hopefully, trying to stimulate her interest a bit.

'Why?'

'The Sargent sketch of Jennie says that was as he first knew her. It was in 1900 that the Sitwells rented 25 Chesham Place from the Moreton Frewens. To have their Sargent painted.'

'So?'

'So at least there is a connection with Sargent and both Jennie and Clara in 1900.' I was beginning to get a little narked.

'Oh, really, Tim. It's all so tenuous.'

'My God! Who was it, standing there in the Tate, with Lord Puddledock or Ribblesdale or whatever staring down at us, who said this was it, this must be it, a painting of the three Jerome sisters? Eh? Who was that?'

'I wish I hadn't, now.'

'Why?'

'I'll tell you why.' She turned to look across at me, full-face. 'Because it's dangerous, that's why. Damned dangerous, Tim. It isn't worth it. It isn't worth any amount of money. It frightens me; attacks and break-ins and murder.'

'Not in England.'

'No? What about our flat?'

'They obviously waited until we were out. Avoided violence.'

'They won't next time!'

'Sue.' I reached across to pat her with one hand but she avoided me and we were doing over a hundred so I had to abandon the attempt. 'Bear with me, please. Just for a day or two more. The quicker I get to Jeremy, the quicker it'll all be over.'

'Ha!'

'It will.'

'Some chance.'

A change of emphasis was needed. Art might help. 'I don't think that you like Sargent very much,' I said. 'I get the feeling that he doesn't turn you on.'

'He doesn't.' She's got firm views, has Sue; only the Impressionists really turn her on. 'He wasn't really an Impressionist, you know.'

'Eh?'

'Some people tried to make out he was one. Because he knew Monet and so on. But Monet always said Sargent wasn't one of them. And Degas was quite contemptuous.'

'Catty lot, artists.'

'I think painting came too easily to him. Sargent, I mean. People were jealous of that. He did experiment with Impressionism, though. Until he painted "Carnation, Lily, Lily, Rose". That's contrary to all the principles of Impressionism. Took him ages to paint it. He had to keep setting the children and lanterns up in the twilight and then rushing out to get a bit of the colour. Made that Broadway lot laugh a bit.'

'I didn't know it was painted in New York?'

'Oh, *Tim*. Really! Russell House, Broadway. He leased it with the Millets. There were a lot of Americans in the Cotswolds then. Sargent went there frequently. Afterwards he took a place at Fladbury. A rectory. That's in Worcestershire as well.'

'Broadway, Worcestershire? The Cotswolds?'

'Yes, yes, of course. What's the matter? Mind that car!'

'Nothing. I thought you said that Sargent only painted in his Tite Street studio? That's why the Sitwells and all those had to go there.'

'Of course. That was for *portraits*.' Her voice was impatient. 'Sargent did lots of *plein-air* paintings, out of doors. He was very good at that. In fact he got to hate portraits. They made his living, a lot of money in fact, but he found it a treadmill. Like your favourite, Orpen. Made Orpen drink himself to death.'

'Did Sargent marry?'

She shot me a glance. 'No, he didn't. But don't get the wrong idea. There's never been a breath of scandal about Sargent. I know your propensity for biographical investigation of that sort.'

'Mmmm. When was he in the Cotswolds?'

'Oh, the eighteen eighties. 'Nineties. That sort of time. Why?'

'Just thinking.'

'Thinking what?'

It was time to stop this, so I quoted:

'Successfully she stopped him drinking,
How can she prevent him thinking?'

'Tim!'

'Sorry. Uncalled for. Do you know that the Frewens had to give up 25 Chesham Place, but they moved into Great Cumberland Place? Number 39A, that was. Shortly after 1900.'

'What are you getting at?'

'Just that Jennie lived at 37A. And Leonie at number 10. So it is entirely possible, given the absence of their menfolk on a regular basis, that the three could have sat for Sargent with ease, round about then.'

'It'd have been a rather mature portrait. Clara would have been fifty.'

'That's no impediment. Sargent often painted mature women, mothers and daughters, that sort of thing. Three famous Americans, at the height of English society, would have been a great subject for him. He painted Jennie's brother-in-law, the Duke of Marlborough, and his wife, Consuelo Vanderbilt, another American, then. He belted out portraits in England and America at an amazing rate. Ah, that reminds me, you do realize that he painted Edward the Seventh – who wanted to knight him but couldn't, because he was an American – and Edward's brother, the Duke of Connaught, as well?'

'Yes. And I know what you're going to say about their relationship with Jennie and Leonie respectively. I've read Anita Leslie too, Tim, remember?'

'Sorry. Ah, we've arrived.'

Jeremy's yacht was parked, or moored, or whatever they call it, in a harbour near Chichester that kept its level against the tide by use of a lock built into a sort of dam, like a breakwater. Within this flooded, peaceful basin, a series of wooden jetties had been constructed so that the yachts could be tied up and yachtsmen could walk on and off them without difficulty. It reminded me a bit of the Connecticut coast, which is full of creeks kitted out the same way. That Saturday afternoon it was relatively empty because most of the berth owners had already set out, anticipating that this would indeed be one of the last glorious weekends of the year, warm and sunny but with a fresh breeze that was ideal for sailing.

I pulled the car to a halt on the earth and gravel near the yacht basin and hopped out. Sue appeared on the other side of the car, pulling on a yellow windcheater against the breeze. The sound of ropes or halyards slapping against metal masts hit my ears. A smell of salt mud, fishy stew and wet boots spiked my nostrils. Big white clouds soared overhead, not obscuring the sun or the blue sky enough to lessen the bright glare and that very clear delineation of detail that you get when, later in the year, the sun is lower on the horizon and seems to pick out every leaf and blade or, in this case, every slapping wavelet and bobbing sea-bird that danced on the water.

'There they are!' Sue pointed and waved. 'There! At the end of the jetty. On their own! Hi! Mary! Jeremy!'

It was true. At the end of the third jetty along to our left stood Jeremy's sloop, preparing to leave. Mary stood on the jetty, holding a rope, preparing to cast off. The throb of the engine, starting up, came over the water.

'Hi!' I roared, running towards them with Sue close behind. 'Hey! Mary! Jeremy! Wait!'

Mary heard us. I saw the flash of her white teeth as she laughed and waved. Her head turned back to Jeremy, half-hidden in the cockpit, and I saw his cap pop up over a coaming. He did something with the controls, and came out over the side. I reached the start of the jetty, but Mary was skipping towards me, lightly hopping over the odd rope across the duckboards.

'Wait!' she called. 'Stay there, Tim! The jetty's very slippery. There's been some spillage.'

I grabbed Sue's arm just as her foot went on to the quay.

'Hold on!' Jeremy bellowed, striding towards us, clad in smart waterproof gear and those light rubber boots with castellated white soles that all that crowd wear. 'Wait there! The jetty's lethally slippery! What on earth are you doing here?'

'The Sargent,' I shrieked back. 'You're not going to believe this, Jeremy. The Sargent. It – '

I didn't hear the next word. My ears went numb. It was like concussion. I could see Jeremy, Mary, Sue's face, their features working, Sue screaming, Mary's eyes white, Jeremy lurching forward, out of control, on to his face in his waterproofs, all in slow motion. I couldn't hear any sound. I saw the yacht rear up in the water, great pieces flying off it, small jagged bits sailing high into the air, water lashing with compression and blast, surfaces churned white by falling debris, rigging and spars and glass and shards going skywards and coming towards us, so that I leapt to hurl Sue and Mary to the ground, trying to cover them as bits clumped down all around us. Sound suddenly returned: a horrible, thudding, banging, screaming sound, air whistling with projectiles, people shouting in fear, birds and gulls shrieking and wheeling. Then silence again.

Sue was having hysterics so I clasped her first. Jeremy, who had a huge mark on his face, was on all fours, shouting at Mary, but she was all right. I got a glance at the remainder of the sloop. There was nothing left above the hull and the hull was missing all one side, so that, with the mooring rope Mary had left in place still holding it, the shattered half was sinking slowly into the water, held by the rope which, obstinately, had not been severed. I realized then that the sloop should not still have been tethered to the jetty. It should have been out on the water, with its crew concentrated in it, in the cockpit, where there would be no escaping the blast, where they would receive the full impact of it. That was how the thing had been timed. Just like the IRA did when they blew up poor old Mountbatten and his family off the west coast of Ireland a few years back.

That was when it came to me. Holding Sue, who was shivering and crying but calming down, and looking at Jeremy's desperate, contorted face as he held his precious Mary to him, safe and sound, the idea of Mountbatten and the IRA triggered back the memory of Mr Goodston's reproving words to me the first time I had visited his shop and made some comment about Anita Leslie and Elizabeth Longford. 'Whenever you are delving into the past – or the present – history or situation of the British Isles, never, but never, neglect what I call the Irish Dimension. Never. It's a fatal mistake.'

That was precisely what I had done. Despite names like O'Hare and Maguire and Casey, I had done just that. As people raced towards us and shouts arose, it hit me that I had completely and utterly neglected the Irish Dimension. Like an absolute fool.

It was time to put that right.

Chapter Sixteen

The Aer Lingus flight from Heathrow to Cork takes off in the mid-afternoon so that, an hour or so later, when you are poised high to the south of that famous Irish city, you can squint out of the plane window to see, even further south, the valley of the River Bandon as it rolls towards Kinsale. On a clear day, when it is not raining, you might discern, far away below you, the village of Innishannon lodged on each bank of the river in a lush setting of superb fishing country.

Mostly, however, it is raining. It certainly was the day Sue and I flew in to Cork, so much so that they said we were lucky to get there at all. The airport had been closed all morning due to low cloud, which meant quite simply that the rain had become dense enough and heavy enough to blot everything out. It lifted briefly during the afternoon, enough for us to land anyway, and then it dropped again, the minute after we landed it seemed to me, so that when Johnson and Perrot handed the hired saloon over to us we had to scurry quickly inside it to avoid getting soaked. We untangled ourselves behind beating wipers that hardly kept the windscreen clear of the sluicing downpour, Sue shaking her wet hair and me pulling my wet trousers off my knees so that rheumatism wouldn't set in.

'I think I'll head straight for Cork,' I said. 'There's no point in going down to Innishannon this evening; everyone will be indoors during weather like this.'

She nodded in agreement and I headed the car

towards town. I'm not sure when it was after the explosion at Chichester that I told Sue I was going to have to go to Ireland. Probably well after she had calmed down and the official inquiries had started, inquiries that got more serious and ominous as each piece of evidence came to light. Jeremy's yacht was not destroyed by a fuel leak or an accident. It was blown up by a bomb, a proper bomb, made from sticks of dynamite and wired to his ignition, his engine ignition, with a timer to ensure that he would be out on the water and exposed to the full force of the blast, as I had guessed. Jeremy was very badly shaken. In all the various problems I've had in the past it has been me, almost uniquely me, with Sue occasionally involved, that has been the target of the violence, and that was what, after Andy's call, I had assumed this time. Jeremy has never had anything directed at him before; the fact that Mary was with him had really rammed the danger home. Jeremy was in London, pondering on the hazards of life with the Art Fund and, after an hysterical and bewildered discussion with me, on the dreadful speculation that someone specifically wanted to do him in. I hoped it wouldn't put Jeremy off the whole enterprise, but I couldn't help being slightly amused; he'd blithely sent me off to pursue the Sargent without hesitation, never suspecting that the boomerang would head in his direction. There was a certain *Schadenfreud* in it all, from my point of view.

Sue had accepted the excursion to Ireland calmly. I was not nearly as calm about her insistence on coming with me, but reason would not prevail.

'Either I come with you,' she said, 'or you don't go.'

'You don't really need to come,' I responded. 'I can

make my inquiries and be back within two days. You could stay with your mother. Or you'd be safe with Nobby and Gillian – '

'No!' Her voice was resolute. 'I will do no such thing. I will come with you. You have had a lucky escape. You have quite fortuitously saved Jeremy and Mary's lives. I believe that this whole thing has acquired a momentum of its own, a force that we must follow. It's like the other things in the past, only this time I feel it more strongly than ever before. I'm not letting you go alone. I don't know what you're looking for and I don't think you're very certain, either, but I'm coming. I said I wouldn't drop out, no matter what happened, and I'm not. You've set this whole train of events in motion and I'm keeping close to you.'

There's no stopping her when she's in that sort of mood and, on quieter reflection, I thought that she would probably be safer with me in Ireland than hanging alone around the flat in London. I booked the tickets and we sallied forth the next day. I'd never been to Cork before and, apart from remembering something vague from my school history books about Desmond and, later, Florence MacCarthy, and the Spanish occupation, and Winston's ancestor John taking the city for King Billy, and how the town always seemed to back the wrong side, the place was a mystery to me. All I knew was that it had the nearest airport to Innishannon, and that we could stay in a good hotel. I also remembered that Moreton Frewen, after staying overlong with Lillie Langtry when bidding a fond farewell to her on leaving for Wyoming, missed his ship in England but caught it at Cork after a Sunday railway chase that had all Ireland betting on the outcome. In those days the

Atlantic steamers stopped at Queenstown, or Cobh, as it is now properly called again, in Cork harbour, before proceeding to America from England. Moreton had to catch the Irish mail train in London, cross to Dublin, hire a special train, race to Cobh, leap on to a sea-going tender and motor out to the departing steamer to be hauled on board by his brother Richard and the hunting party because his overnight farewell had caused him to miss his proper embarkation. All in a day's adventure to the cool-headed Moreton, who must have known Cork well from his youthful days at Innishannon.

The city was grey and watery as we came into the old, historic centre with the many bridges over the Lee and found our way to the hotel. A silver-grey BMW nearly collided with me as I altered course down St Patrick's Street, admiring the quays as I crossed the bridge. In the continuous rain it wasn't easy to be certain I had the right way and I called an apology after the vanishing German car as I turned again into MacCurtain Street, but the driver wouldn't have heard me. We unloaded our cases and were welcomed into the warmth, where an Irish whiskey and a splendid meal of fresh fish soon dispelled thoughts of the damp outside.

Sue was excited. She was almost feverish. She talked animatedly, she ate ravenously, she insisted on going out for a walk round the town in what had now become a drizzle, she clutched at me in enthusiasm, she was like a terrier nearing the end of a burrow for a rabbit. I realized that she had the nervous antici-pation of someone approaching the end of a quest, someone convinced that a great quarry was in sight. Since I wasn't sure myself quite what my own instincts had brought me to, I tried to be a calming influence without dampening her, but it was difficult, with her on such a high key, not to be drawn into an enthusiastic reaction myself. Especially when the effect upon her, after we had retired for the night, was of an order that I won't embarrass anyone by describing. I've often pondered, in those gloomy moments that one gets, whether my attraction for Sue is due more to the excitement of the Art Fund's occasionally hair-raising acquisitions than to my scintillating personality, but it doesn't do to dwell on such introspective doubts. The fact is that of Cork itself I retain an affectionate, damply-grey memory, but the night that we spent there will never fade from my mind.

Mornings of joy are supposed to give for evenings of tearfulness. This time it was the other way round. The next day was cloudy but it wasn't raining. I woke with grave doubts in my mind. Sue gave me a rapturous embrace, leapt from the bed and practically drove me from the room in excitement. We had a splendid breakfast in which the local Cork-cured bacon and soda bread figured richly. I wondered what the hell I thought I was doing. I had terrible presentiments, irrational superstitious fears. Mr Goodston's warnings sounded in my head. We were in Ireland, we were here to dig up the past, we were going to intrude. Uncontrollable forces might be let loose. Sue golloped down the biggest breakfast I've ever seen her eat. She didn't seem to notice my qualms.

'Golly, I was hungry,' she exclaimed, giving me a flash of her blue eyes. 'Isn't this terrific? I feel marvellous! It must be the air. Come on, we've got to get going, haven't we? Mustn't waste time. Will we go on up north to Monaghan afterwards? To Castle

Leslie? Buck up, Tim, I've finished. Drink up your tea.'

We got out on to the road, back past the airport, on to Ballinhassig and, with the signposts pointing to Bandon, we soon arrived at Innishannon, with a fork to the left down towards Kinsale.

There wasn't anything there. Nothing at all.

Oh, of course, I knew that the house had been burnt down by the Republicans in 1921. I knew that. I knew how the Frewens came to own the place before Moreton was born, taking it over from the improvident Adderleys in return for a loan of £60,000 which could never be repaid. I knew how old Thomas Frewen, Moreton's father, had grumbled about good Sussex money lost on an Irish village, but had none the less been a conscientious landlord and repaired all the houses, maintained all the culverts, walls and drains, replanted the woods. I knew how Moreton had come here to learn all about salmon fishing as a boy of twelve. I knew how he had inherited the estate when his brother Richard was drowned while yachting off the Pembroke coast. I knew how he had tried to breed trout and raise quail in this densely vegetated, heavily-poached, richly endowed countryside. I knew how Clara preferred her beloved Brede Place in Sussex, never understanding Ireland. I knew how their children had loved Innishannon, as Moreton had, and how their daughter Clare, who married Wilfred Sheridan and was quickly widowed by the First World War, had come back in 1922 and climbed the garden wall to look at the blackened ruin of their old home, just as I, now, was sitting here, sixty-four years later, wondering what the hell I was doing in this remote, damp and beautiful place with the green hills and rocky walls and fisherman's river all around me.

What I did first, after stopping to reflect on events and to try and stifle my misgivings, was to go to the Innishannon House Hotel. I thought it was the Frewens' old place, rebuilt, but it wasn't. It was an old house all right, 1720 the brochures said, right spang on the river, with smooth green lawns and arched loggia windows, but it wasn't the Frewens'. The proprietor was called Brian Macarthy and he grinned sympathetically at me and Sue as we stood before him.

'Oh no,' he said. 'This isn't it. The Frewens took over the Adderleys' place – ' he spoke as if it were yesterday – 'and pulled it down to build a new house in the early nineteenth century. Riverview, I think it was called. It was burnt down in what we here euphemistically call the troubles. It's on the north side of the river, down a side road by the Catholic Church.'

'Is there anything left of it?'

He shook his head. 'No, I don't think so. It's a while since I last looked, but it was crumbled then and ivy grew all over the place. There's a modern house built in front of it. Clare Sheridan used to say how like the jungle it is round here. The vegetation grows like mad and covers everything so quickly. The whole place was encumbered, you know. To Barclays Bank. They still own a few houses in the village. There's a tradition that Winston Churchill came here because he was Frewen's nephew, but I don't know if that's true.' He smiled inquiringly. 'Are you members of the family? One of Moreton Frewen's grandsons was here a while back. From Australia, I think.

Part of the Anglo-Irish diaspora, you might say. The British diaspora, indeed.'

I shook my head, warming to him. 'No, we're not members of the family. We're just doing some research. On, er, the family and its associations. Is there anything left of the trout hatchery?'

He shook his head vigorously. 'Indeed not. I'm afraid they did for that straight away. There were some very bloody-minded people about just then, you know. The fish bailiff – he was a Scot, I believe – was done for at the same time.' He smiled, the shy, apologetic smile of the Irishman trying to break the news gently to the English that things had been very nasty in our direction but that he really meant us well personally, even if in his heart of hearts he felt we might have deserved it.

'Is there anyone left in the village who remembers the house?' Sue was still eager, anxious. 'Anyone who worked there or anything?'

'Ach, no, I don't think so.' He smiled at her tolerantly. 'It was a long time ago, you know. Nineteen-twenty-one. People have moved on and they'd be in their eighties now, or have been children at the time.' His expression changed. 'Now that's a thought. There was a fellow called Coughlan worked at the hatchery. His son's a poacher, towards Macroom. I've heard that he would remember the Frewens but I've never met him. He's a bit of a legend as a salmon poacher – they're a breed round here – being brought up on the Bandon, but he's a very suspicious sort of an old man. A recluse, almost.' He scratched his chin dubiously. 'He might talk to you. Do you want me to see if I can find his address?'

'Oh, Mr Macarthy!' Sue hopped from one leg to

the other. 'Please! Please! If you could! We'd be so grateful.'

He grinned attractively and looked at her eyes, sparkling with excitement. 'How could a man resist that, now? Wait here and I'll see what I can find out.'

I sat down on a hall chair as he disappeared into his office. Ivy and a tangle of shrubbery had grown over material relics of the Frewens here. The only traces that remained were people's memories, laughing references to improvidence and wildness, distant fated activities that bore no relation to this world. I thought of the trails I had followed before, to Somers Town and Meudon, to Hastings and Hove and Bedford Park on similar pursuits, with similar instincts. I remembered Small Hythe where there wasn't anything to find, either; E. W. Godwin was just as evanescent as the tall, handsome, hunting Frewen of such financial mayhem. Here I was, doing the same sort of thing again, for the remote passing chance of a celebrated painting that somehow didn't seem to get any nearer. There was nothing of me here; this was a delightful foreign country where Englishmen like me no longer belonged, had no presence, were part of an uncomfortably-near unpleasant past, even if welcomed unreservedly as tourists, remote relations, by genuinely smiling people.

I was wrong. About my lack of presence, anyway.

'What a shame.' Sue's voice cut into my thoughts. 'They must have loved it here. Look at this super country hotel. I can understand why all the Frewens were so keen to come. It must have been a bitter blow. But they weren't the only ones. Lord Bandon was kidnapped and Castle Bernard was burnt down.'

'Mmmm?'

'You're lost, aren't you?'

'What?'

'You're lost. I can tell.' Her tone was decisive, still full of electric enthusiasm. 'Come on, Tim, buck up! This old chap Coughlan may have the answers. If not, we'll go to Monaghan.'

'I don't know. I feel apprehensive.'

'Oh, Tim! You of all people. I – ah, here's Mr Macarthy.'

He looked dubiously at a piece of paper as he came towards us, across the hall. 'I've tried to draw a map,' he explained. 'You have to take the Cookstown road from Bandon and then head towards Macroom. But it's a difficult place, up a country track. And there's no phone, of course.' He gave Sue the paper apologetically. 'I hope you can make sense of that. I got the directions from an old village woman but I can't vouch that they'll be right. You know how it is in Ireland; everyone knows the way but no one ever gets there.'

We laughed with him and, promising to return, we got back into the car. I drove back on to the Bandon road, just noticing the silver flash of a saloon turning by the Catholic Church as we sped our way past a roadside shrine set back in the loose stone wall bordering the route. It made me think of my near-collision the night before in the pouring rain, the symbolic sense of being partly lost, partly navigating by instinct, that comes over me from time to time. Fortunately Sue interrupted any further thoughts with peremptory directions of a practical nature, so I had to concentrate on the specific way ahead.

We had to ask for directions twice. There was a smaller road, signposted only in Gaelic, which made life a bit difficult. Then there was a direction which seemed to be doubling us back on ourselves. Finally, at right angles to a side road to Macroom, a rutted track between two rough stone walls, buttressed by banks of nettles and vetches, led up a long green slope that steepened as it curved upwards towards a distant cottage. Reluctantly I turned the hired saloon up the track. The cottage was a fairly typical Irish one, of a single storey, thatched, with a chimney perched on the top of each thick, gabled end-wall. In the centre of the whitewashed front was a door, with a small window on each side. A thin whisper of blue smoke dribbled out of the right-hand chimney and vanished into the damp breeze. Behind the cottage loomed rounded hills and, as we painfully lurched over the stony bumps between the walls, I could see short, stunted trees half-circling the flat space behind the building. The track levelled off a bit near the house and I could see that it carried the single stony way onwards, past the cottage and over the hill to some unknown destination out on the wet windy hills above the lusher vegetation of the sheltered valleys.

I pulled the car up outside the stone cottage and drew the vehicle off the track on to a bumpy green verge. Getting out into the quick breeze, I noticed how much closer we were to the clouds that drove across above us, and how much barer the world seemed to be up here, scrubbed by the wind. Water trickled out of the stone wall bordering the road, crossed the track and disappeared into the wall the other side, parting the nettles with a flat, wet, muddy groove. Above the low stones there was a fine distant view over green fields and wooded cloughs that must have contained more streams, rivers, and fast-running water bubbling over rocks. A fine prospect for a fish poacher, I thought, as I walked to the front door with Sue at my side.

No one answered my knock. I tried again and waited. Sue looked up meaningfully at the bit of smoke coming from the chimney but it was probably a peat fire of the sort they keep going all day. After a while I gave it up and tramped round the side of the cottage to recce the back, in case there was anyone there. I turned the corner of the building and pulled up quickly, short in my tracks.

An old man stood before me, braced with his legs apart among the vegetables clinging to the ground in that windswept back garden. Across his arm, with the ease of long habitude, lay an old-fashioned shotgun, a twelve-bore, smooth and polished with the wear of decades. On his head was a cloth cap, greasy with age. He was wrapped in an ancient, oiled coat of antique cut, with huge flapped pockets for game and pouches for ammunition. The face was lined, deeply weathered, shrewd and sharp, like a creature of the forest, heath or hedgerow. Very keen eyes, narrowed by ages of frowning into the weather, peered out from under spiky white eyebrows. His gaze flicked as Sue came round the side of the cottage behind me and she stopped, hesitant, to look at me. I realized that his positioning was careful and that the shotgun, though broken open, was charged with the necessary two cartridges. No one could have come round the side of that cottage and taken him by surprise. No one could have avoided his field of fire; he had a clear view of anyone trying to flank round the back of the house. He must have watched the car come all the way up the track, watched us get out and knock at his door, waited to see how keen we were to find him.

'Mr Coughlan?' I stood up straight, kept my face open, my voice as pleasant as possible. My arms were by my sides.

'I am,' he said.

His voice was quiet and middle-toned, without the hardness of Dublin or the north. Somehow I felt a confidence that this man would listen to me, had a natural sympathy that wouldn't tell me to get lost, like so many people might.

'I'm sorry to bother you. I'm from England. I got your name from the hotel in Innishannon.'

'From England.' It was a statement, not a question. 'I understand that.'

'And this, er, this is a friend of mine, Sue Westerman. My name is Tim Simpson. We came to find you.'

'Simpson.' He seemed to muse slightly over the name. 'You're not a Scotsman, then?'

'No. I'm English. From London.'

Silence. He was waiting for me. I cleared my throat. 'I was told you might be able to help me. It's a matter concerning the time the Frewens owned the house at Innishannon.'

'The Frewens?'

'Yes. Moreton Frewen, actually.'

'That's a long time ago.'

'Yes. It is.'

'I was only eleven years old when they burnt that house down.'

'Er, I suppose so. But I believe your father worked there for a while?'

'My father worked there for thirty years.'

I didn't seem to be getting anywhere. He was staring at me in an odd way that was disconcerting. I was wondering whether it might be a good idea to get Sue to talk to him, Irishmen being particularly charming with the ladies, when he spoke again.

'You must forgive me for staring like this, but have I not seen you somewhere before?'

That flummoxed me. 'No. Er, no. I don't think so.'

'I never forget a face.' His own brown, crinkled features moved with a thoughtful, friendly look. 'I said to myself as you came round the house, I said that feller with the broken nose, I know him now, I've seen him before.'

'Really? I don't think so. I've never been here before.'

'I said to myself he's not a boxer, not the way he moves. If you'll pardon me, I know the way people move, it's like animals d'you see, you can tell from how an animal moves what it does, what it has to do to live, and it's the same with people.'

'Oh.' This is absurd, I thought, I'm standing in the middle of a vegetable garden at the back of an Irish bothy, probably on a wild goose chase, time's going by, and I'm not a step nearer, it –

'Rugby, now. That'll be a rugby player, I said to myself. Was I right? I'll never make a mistake about a thing like that. Will I?'

'You're right. I used to be a rugby player, but I haven't been for years.'

'Ah, but it leaves a mark, d'you see? A forward now, you'd be a forward. Wouldn't you?'

'I was. How did you know?'

A wide smile of pure joy came over his face. 'Ah, sir, 'tis unmistakable. Quite entirely unmistakable. My nephew, d'you see, he was a rugby forward. He played in England, too. To the pride of his entire family. After he left Cork. He'd be about your age, now.'

'Oh, really? I'm afraid I can't recall, er, any Coughlan in my time. Who did he play for?'

'His name wouldn't be Coughlan. He was my sister's boy. She married a Horrigan, from Cork.'

'Horrigan? I can't – Good God! You're not talking of Mad Paddy Horrigan, the lock forward? Played for London Irish? Massive great bloke?'

The old man drew himself up in reproachful dignity. He shot me a look of grave affront. 'My nephew Patrick did indeed play for the London Irish side. With great distinction. After taking his medical degree.'

'About ten years ago? Maybe twelve?'

'Now I know it! I know it!' The old fellow slapped his thigh, making the shotgun bounce and me jerk. 'I know where I've seen you! It's in the photograph. I've got it inside. It was an anniversary match –'

'Oh, no! Don't tell me. O'Shaughnessy's XV versus the London Irish. An invitation side, at Richmond? They scooped me in at the last moment because they were short of a tight-head prop. Eleven years ago, it was. There was a photo afterwards. My God, Paddy was a powerful bug – er, fellow, he really was. A shocker to try and stop. Nearly broke my collar-bone.'

'Simpson! That's your name! You're in my house. My house right here. I remember Patrick spoke of you. If only that eejit Lacey hadn't asked that Englishman to join him, he said, we'd have done a lot better. He was forever blocking my way.'

'That was a match! And my God, afterwards! They destroyed nearly the whole of Soho. At one stage they got the chorus line from one of the musicals – *Hair*, I think it was, mind you, it might have been *Oh, Calcutta!* – and the girls – no, Sue's looking at me, I'd better not. What a small world!'

'But look at this! What will you think of me? Keeping you standing out here in this godforsaken vegetable garden in this keen wind without a thought of asking you inside? And you here all the way from England. It's disgraceful. I'm getting old, but it's no excuse. Come in, come in. No, dear lady, not the back door. I'm ashamed of that, it's such a mess. The front, if you please.'

He shepherded us back round to the front of the cottage and threw the door open with a flourish. We entered a dark but brightly-polished room with a deep fireplace, in which a peat fire smouldered dully. He put the shotgun down carefully on the butt inside the nook and snapped it shut, cartridges and all. I hoped the safety-catch still worked.

'Here we are!' he crowed, taking down a mounted photograph from a rank of them that lapped each other all along the mantel ledge framing the top of the fireplace. 'The names are all written on the back. I've looked through all these evening after evening. There's no telly here, you see. Thank the Lord.'

It was still quite fresh and bright. A black-and-white picture of a crowd of muddy rugby players, splashed and tattered, grinning cheerfully at the camera. Sue's hair brushed the side of my neck as I looked at it and I heard her laugh softly. 'My, but you were younger then. What a dreadful thug you look! How on earth did you come to play in such a match?'

I grinned at her and the old man. 'I was having a quiet beer in a pub on the Sunbury Road and four of O'Shaughnessy's side came in on their way to the match. I'd played with one of them at Cambridge. Tony Lacey, he was called, and he gave a great shout and said, "Tim, you're just the man we need, we're short of a prop for the match." The next thing I knew I was on the rugger field full of beer, with twenty-nine Irishmen knocking six bells out of each other and me the English punchbag in the middle. Shocking, it was, but they were a great crowd.' I stabbed my finger close to the group photograph. 'There's Paddy, er, your nephew Patrick. Cor, he was a big fellow. What's he doing now?'

The old man smiled happily. 'He's in Australia. He has a partnership in a medical practice there. Owns his own racehorse. He was always a fine boy and he still writes to me from time to time.'

'Send him my best, then. I didn't know him well, but I remember him vividly.'

'I will, for sure. Please have a seat. Let me give you a cup of tea? The young lady can use one, I'm sure?'

'Oh, Mr Coughlan – ' Sue was at her most seductive – 'it'll be a lot of trouble, won't it? Please don't bother.'

'Of course it won't. Look – is the kettle not practically boiling on the hob already? A cup of Irish tea will warm you on a day like this. And an old man doesn't often get the chance of such fair company in his house.'

She blushed prettily and thanked him. It's a good job he's not forty years younger, I thought, otherwise there'd be problems, but he was putting teacups together and looking at me curiously as I sat at his cottage table in that simple but clean living-room. He picked up a fan of rook's feathers to liven the fire with, and spoke thoughtfully.

'Moreton Frewen, now. He and his brother Richard – they were fine men with guns and horses. Great tall fellers, my father said, when they were young they'd ride over anything. Wild, mad as hares, they were. Do anything for a bet on a race. All Ireland gambled on whether Moreton would catch the steam packet to America when he raced to catch it at Cork on a special train from Dublin.' He winked at me. 'The tale was that it was Mrs Langtry who'd detained him and caused him to miss the boat in England.'

'It's true.'

'Ha, I thought it was. They were wild all right.' He cocked an eye at me. 'My nephew Patrick was something of a prankster, you may say, but he had nothing on the Frewens. They were half-Irish, you know.'

I nodded. 'Their mother was a Homan, from County Kildare.'

'That's so. A tiny little woman, my father said.'

I tried to say it as gently as I could. 'Which made it all the harder for Moreton to understand.'

'What?'

'That they burnt his house down. It hit him hard. The Frewens were good landlords. Old Thomas Frewen spent a fortune on Innishannon. The village, I mean. Moreton loved the place. It hit him hard. He was an MP here once.'

'It hit him hard. Him?' Old Coughlan's eyes pierced mine. 'I remember the night it happened, young man! My father came in, crying. In tears, he was. I was eleven years old. I'd never seen my father cry. I was brought up to be a brave little boy, not to cry and all that. And there was my father, crying. "Sure," he said, "we're destroyed entirely now. The house has gone. And everything in it. The Frewens'll never come back to us. It's finished for us. The trout hatchery will go, and the quails, the partridges and the pheasants. What will become of us?" They were terrible times. My father kept his shotgun – that very shotgun there – always to hand. He advised me to do the same and I always have. I'm ashamed to say that's life in Ireland and it isn't any better now. What with the economic troubles and the young folk all leaving once again and Haughey bound to get in at the next election because Fitzgerald, poor man, is too quiet for all of us.'

His eyes dropped and I shuffled my feet. 'I'm sorry. I didn't mean to open old wounds.'

'Ach, in Ireland you can't avoid it.' He gave me a faint smile. 'Let's be having our tea.'

The kettle, on an iron stand or trivet half into his peat fire, started to steam and spit. He stooped to lift it off with a thick pad and poured boiling water into an ancient brown teapot, filling it to the top so that leaves bobbed on the surface and a herbal, fragrant smell vapoured up to our nostrils before he dropped a stained lid over the brew.

'A fine strong cup o' tea,' he said. 'There's nothing like it.'

I stared at the photograph over the mantelpiece. Which philosopher can ever explain the consequences of our actions? As a result of that hilarious beer in a pub on the Sunbury Road eleven years ago, my photograph was lodged here, in this remote, isolated corner of Ireland, preserved, as the poet says, smaller and clearer as the years go by, to stare out in the blurred, youthful, cheerful ignorance of that day. Where else might my younger visage look unknowingly on the daily life of some family or pensioner, guardians of a favourite son or nephew's sporting past? Probably nowhere; this was an Irish experience, the sort of thing that only happens to you in Ireland, on Irish days, with Irish people.

'Has it given you a turn?' Old Coughlan gave me a knowing smile and a lift of his eyebrows. 'Will it not be something to tell your grandchildren one day? Ye walked into a cottage in Ireland and find your picture on the wall? Hey, that's a thing, now. A thing to tell your grandchildren?' He winked at Sue, who winked back at him like a true colleen.

'It certainly will be. It's quite extraordinary. I don't know how to describe it. The most peculiar feeling.'

'Ha! The tea'll have pulled nicely, now. I'll pour it out. 'Twas fate, that's what it was. That brought you here, I mean. There's always an explanation for such things. There has to be. Will that be enough milk for you? It was destiny for sure. Say when, now, dear lady.'

'Super.'

'And you, sir?'

'Fine. Thanks.'

'There's too much we can't explain, so why bother trying? It'll all be clear one day, I've always said, but in the meantime look after yourself, look after yourself carefully. That's the thing.'

The tea was hot and powerful, restoring my slightly jaded metabolism to a more alert condition. The old man regarded me placidly, showing no desire to hurry the conversation or to inquire what it was that I had wanted with him. Sue, sensitive to mood as ever, had dropped into a quiet calm, sipping her tea and rubbing one foot gently down the back of her leg in a sort of soothing motion. The cottage room was warm and peaceful, its thick walls insulated the interior from the weather. I cleared my throat.

'Have you been away from Innishannon for a long time? Living here, I mean?'

'Oh yes. During the Troubles me father got a job in Kinsale. Then in Cork. He didn't like it; he was a countryman, d'you see. So we moved out to this region and he rented a little farm and then I did the same. So here I am. It's a simple story. I've never missed anything I wanted here.'

'Do you remember the big house at Innishannon? The Frewens' place?'

'Of course I do. I was eleven when it went. A boy's memory is always bright. It's a man's you can't rely on.' His eyes crinkled for a moment at his own wisdom and he sipped his tea. 'What was it you were looking for? If it's not an impertinent question?'

'A painting.' I'd decided to be direct. 'A painting of the three sisters. Mrs Frewen and her two sisters.'

His eyes widened and he almost glared at me for a moment before I realized that I had really given him a big surprise. He put his tea down on the scrubbed wooden table-top and looked from me to Sue and then back to me again.

'Now how the devil – pardon me, dear lady – but how the very devil did you know about that?'

Sue put her tea down and I sensed her tensing with excitement. I put a hand on her arm. 'I guessed it, mostly. But Frewen himself – Moreton, I mean – he made a note about it. Someone we know found the note.'

'Well I'll be damned! Indeed I will. I thought I was the only one left who knew about that.'

'You saw it? Was it hanging on the wall?'

He shook his head vigorously. 'Indeed it was not! It certainly never hung on any wall! It was a secret, was it not? A dire family secret. It was kept completely out of sight. That's how I saw it.'

'I beg your pardon?'

'It was covered over. It was in the top attic, right up in the roof. There was a scandal connected with it. I would never have been seeing it if I hadn't been a harum-scarum lad. We were always up to pranks. We used to play hide-and-seek all over. Up in the attics, sometimes, but the family and the servants, they used to give us a real hiding if they caught us.'

'But you saw it?' Sue was too excited to wait.

'Oh, dear lady, let me tell you, now. One day it was raining like hell, as it always does here in March, and my father was down at the trout hatchery doing something and I was bored, so I sneaked in the house for a piece of bread and butter from the cook. Drunk as a lord she was, brandy was her tipple, and while she wasn't looking I sneaked up the back stairs – all the big houses had a servants' staircase – and up I went, up and up, higher and higher, till I thought I'd reached heaven. But it wasn't, you see. It was the very top attic. I'd never been there before, the door was stiff with damp and dust and I could only just push it open a crack. But I was a thin wiry lad and I squeezed through and there were papers and boxes all strewn about. And a big frame with a cloth over it. So I pulled the cloth to one side and there they were, three angels they seemed. I really thought I was in heaven then, with them ladies in old-fashioned dresses looking at me. I found afterwards that was how they dressed before the war, with long clothes and folds and ribbons and things, but I didn't know then. And I asked my father that evening if rich folk always had angels up in the attic and he gave me a hiding like I'd never had. I howled so loud my mother cried and he was sorry. He really was. He took me in his arms and said he was sorry. Then he said I mustn't tell anyone, not a single soul, what I had seen, it would be bad luck, there was a curse and we'd all be ruined if I breathed a word. So I promised, of course.'

'Good grief. But you're sure it was the three of them? The sisters?'

'Oh sure. I recognized Mrs Frewen at once. She was younger, mind. They were in different poses, like, it's hard to describe, and I only saw them the once. But I eavesdropped on my parents afterwards, because my father had to comfort my mother, d'you see, for the hiding he'd given me. I crept down out of bed. I was fascinated and I listened to them from behind the door.'

'What did they say?'

'Ah well. I was a lad, you know, and it were hard to understand these grown-up things. As far as I could understand it, there was a scandal about the painting. I don't know what, something to do with who paid for it, and one of the ladies' husbands was angry so it was put away in Innishannon for safety and to be out of sight. To be forgotten.'

'And so it was. Right up to the fire?'

'Oh, for sure. It went up with the house, God save us, although the roof and part of the wall fell out from that attic side, my father said, throwing papers and burning bits all over the garden. The painting went all right, because afterwards he found the charred pieces of frame and the black bits of canvas were still sticking to it. When they were clearing up the rubbish they found that. That was the end of it. My father was like a broken man anyway. It was a terrible time. They murdered the fish bailiff and my father took us away quickly too, first to Kinsale and then to Cork. Ah, it's hard in Ireland and it always has been. They were terrible times and the North's no better now. The Leslies, they're in County Monaghan, right up on the border, and my father always thought the painting might have something to do with them, with Lady Leonie anyway, but he never had time to find out. It's a strange thing, you coming all the way here to ask me this, you and your photograph here all the time. It's a day for picture stories now, isn't it? Fate it is, for sure.'

I found that I was staring at him with a fixed intensity that hurt my eyeballs and turned to look at Sue. She had an expression on her face that possibly only Ireland could induce. The mixture of emotions would have been laughable if I hadn't been near to exploding myself.

'Three million dollars,' I said at last. 'Bits of charred frame and ash. Strewn all over the garden.'

'The painting. That beautiful painting.' Her eyes fixed on mine. 'Just like the Wyndhams, I'll bet. It may not be my favourite, but he was a fine painter. And that particular painting – I can't believe it. A wonderful work of art.'

'Oh dear.' Old Coughlan looked anxiously at us both. 'Sure I've upset you, now. Me and my – no, to be fair, I've never told anyone about that picture, not for donkey's and donkey's years. To think that you'd come all this way only to be disappointed. Isn't that a shame?'

'Mr Coughlan, you've been so kind.' Sue put a hand on his arm. 'It's not fair of us to spoil your story. It was a wonderful story. We're really grateful to you for telling us.'

'But –'

'No buts. It's helped to settle a long argument. To lay a ghost. And I'm sure you're right about Fate bringing us here. What an extraordinary experience it's been.' She smiled into his anxious eyes. 'Tim's photo and everything. We'll never forget that. The painting's only history, now, Mr Coughlan. Only history.'

'Oh, Ireland's got enough of that.'

'How right you are. I'm sorry, but could I have some more of this delicious tea? It really has done me good.'

'But of course!' His anxious eyes brightened and he got to his feet. 'I'll give the pot a boost right away. What about you, sir?'

'Tim, Mr Coughlan. My name is Tim. I'd love another cup, thank you. I rather feel I need it.'

He smiled at that and bustled about with the pot. It boiled again presently and he refilled our cups in triumph. I felt a sense of exhausting anti-climax, of unreality, but Sue was terrific in that situation. She drew old Coughlan out and chatted to him brightly, so that he soon was telling her all about the game and the garden and how the fish were to be caught. I thought of the car outside and the flights to London, and the way the sky was going grey in the way that it does when rain threatens in County Cork. I thought about Jeremy and the Art Fund, dead Perkins, pieces of picture frame and charred canvas, the Whitney exhibition, Lord Ribblesdale, and beautiful women painted wearing their expensive dresses in rooms with high ceilings. I heard the compressive thud of Jeremy's yacht going for a Burton, Jeremy shouting, pieces of wreckage cascading down. I saw the face of the lumber-jacketed man at O'Hare, my fists hitting him, violence, destruction. Mortal ruin.

'We've lost him,' old Coughlan said, and I realized he was talking of me.

'I'm sorry. Very sorry. I was miles away.'

'Ah well, have I not given you something to think about? Sometimes it's better not to bother with history. Some stories are best left untold.'

Sue was looking at me reprovingly for my manners. I smiled and thanked the old man again. 'We must be going. I'm eternally grateful to you. For closing a chapter for us. At least our minds will be at rest after this. Now that we know.'

'You're welcome. Of course you are very welcome. And come back, won't you? You can have a fine holiday here in the summer. I'll show you all the finest places. I'll have some fine salmon for you. Will you not come?'

'We will. We promise we'll come back.' Sue smiled brightly. 'Won't we, Tim?'

'Of course. And give my best to Pad — er, your nephew, Patrick, when you next write.'

The old man grinned. 'I'll do that, right enough. And remind him of his nickname. It's a few years since I heard it.'

'Sorry about that.'

'No offence. He was a wild boy all right.'

We went out through the low front door into the greying light outside and shook hands with him. We were moving towards the car when Sue stopped. Another car was coming up the long, stone-walled track towards the cottage. It was a bright silver BMW. It bumped its way carefully towards us with great caution, the tinted windows reflecting back the whitish-grey daylight and dark clouds, so that you couldn't see the driver's face. I couldn't have got our hired car past it, so I stood outside the cottage and took Sue's arm as I watched the BMW approach. Old Coughlan disappeared inside.

As the car got closer I could see that there were two men in it. Near to the cottage it stopped. I heard the driver put the hand-brake on. The engine was still running.

The passenger door opened and a man with gold-rimmed spectacles got out. I recognized the spare figure and dark hair of Alexander Carlton. He didn't smile or greet me; he stood a pace or two away from the BMW, closer to us, and stared at me. The driver's door opened and another man got out. I'd never seen him before. He was stocky and square, with very light hair. He had a machine-pistol in his hand and pointed it at me as he walked round the front of the car to stand closer to Carlton. Sue gave a small cry and then closed her mouth. I held her arm tightly.

'I'm afraid it's all been for nothing, Alex,' I said. 'The painting got burnt with the house. The Frewen luck again.'

His face was intent and serious. 'How do you know?'

'I guessed it. That's why I came here. But old Mr Coughlan, in there, has confirmed it. His father saw the bits after the fire. The Sargent was kept hidden in the attic.'

'Was it the three Jerome sisters?'

'Yes, it was. I'd forgotten that you studied in Florence as well as the other places. Sargent was born there. Has he always been an obsession with you?'

'Not an obsession. A lifetime study.'

'Must have given you a shock when I talked about it, all innocently, at the first board meeting. Shouldn't you be in Chicago, by the way?'

He didn't reply. He seemed to be thinking.

'You've been after it for years, I suppose?'

He still didn't answer.

'Well, it's too late now.' I began to feel garrulous, light-headed. 'It's gone. Since 1921.' I was repeating myself, trying to prompt a reaction. The light-haired man still held the pistol pointed at us. Sue made an involuntary movement and I restrained her. 'It's gone, Alex.'

'Oh no it hasn't,' he said oddly, still staring at me with that bare-eyed look his glasses gave him.

'I'm afraid it has. Old Coughlan can confirm that.'

'Only he can. And you. An English couple, snooping, and an old salmon poacher. Not likely to cause much excitement in Ireland.'

'Why? You've nothing to gain now.'

His face still showed no emotion. 'If I authenticate a Sargent, it will stand at auction. Whenever it was painted.' He turned his head towards the light-haired man.

'Stay clear of the door,' I said to Sue. 'Move to your left.'

'Kill them.' Carlton's voice was unemotional.

The fair-haired man raised the pistol slightly as I hurled myself round Sue, to the left, leaving the doorway clear. The blast made Sue scream. My heart nearly burst all its blood-vessels but the fair-haired man took the charge of shot right in the face. As he went bloodily backwards, the machine-pistol flew across to Carlton's side and he leapt for it, shouting. I had a fearsome glimpse of him bending, turning towards us with the weapon in his hands, screaming. Then the second blast burst his features horribly. I saw shattered gold spectacles, splashed with blood, circle through the air to fall into a clump of nettles beside a stone wall.

Old Coughlan stepped out of the doorway, breaking his shotgun open smoothly as he brought two more cartridges out of his pocket. 'I knew that was bad news as soon as I saw the car,' he said. 'A BMW is always bad news in Ireland.' He snapped the shotgun shut again. 'They'll be from the North, I suppose?'

Chapter Seventeen

'I don't quite understand.' Sue spoke quietly as I eased the Jaguar out of the London suburbs to the south-east. 'Why it is that you want to go to this Northiam place.'

'To lay a ghost. The ghost of Moreton Frewen.'

'I should have thought that you'd had quite enough of that gentleman. Now that the whole thing's settled you ought, surely, to be glad to let sleeping dogs lie.'

We had been back for several days. Ireland was sinking into unreal memory, distant, unconnected, another place. Another place so far from London, so different and remote, that the memories had a dream-like quality, as I imagine a veteran's memories of war experience must become: remote yet real, distant yet intensely personal. I won't tire you with all the explanations that the Garda of County Cork had had to have. It felt as though it would take forever. I had to explain how old Coughlan had defended us superbly, how there was no doubt about Carlton's intentions, how the whole incident had come about. Days passed, days during which the Garda contacted the whole world to check our story. We were politely treated but confined to our hotel until, finally, we were allowed to leave and assured that old Coughlan would not be charged. Back in London, I was at a loose end. Everyone connected with the Bank and Christerby's was so shocked and horrified that they seemed to be avoiding me. Jeremy was immensely relieved and quite congratulatory, for him. The loss of the Sargent was tempered by the safety of his situation, now that the danger was over. Jeremy had visibly mixed emotions.

Corroborative evidence started to come in from all quarters. According to Andy Casey, the Chicago police knew of the light-haired man; he was a professional killer. Loose ends were being steadily tied up. Sue and I had been lying low in Onslow Gardens, Sue recovering from a terrifying experience but for which, as before, she accepted some responsibility due to her own decisions. The weather was still weakly sunny, but much cooler. It seemed to me that any visit to Frewen's birth and burial place I was going to make had better be made right away, to get the whole thing over and done with. The climate didn't incline me to dawdle; I headed into Sussex at a purposeful speed.

'What else have they come up with about Carlton?' Sue demanded, after a while. 'I mean, I can understand the greed for money, especially in an expert who saw everyone else making fortunes that made his salary look puny, but it still doesn't explain it completely. Not to me, anyway.'

'Sargent was an obsession with Carlton. I never realized that until the very end. I knew that Carlton had studied in Florence, which is where Sargent was born. His parents toured Europe, permanently separated from America in an interminable search for health. But who hasn't studied in Florence these days? That was no criterion. Then Carlton had studied in Paris. Sargent learnt his craft there, in Carolus-Duran's atelier. So what? Who hasn't studied in Paris, either? Or London? I mean, every darned art boffin from here to Alaska has trailed round all three. Throw in Venice and Carlton might have become a Whistler freak. As it was, it seems he spent a lot of time in Boston, looking at Sargent's murals for the Public Library. He spent all his spare time tracking down every painting and portrait he could record. I've no doubt he knew all about the charcoal sketch of Lady Randolph Churchill at an early stage; how he found out about the three Jerome sisters being painted together is something we'll never know. He wanted that painting for emotional reasons as much as for the money.'

'Yuk. He hired those criminals. That killer. Those thugs who attacked you at O'Hare. I suppose that vile pale man with the gun killed poor Perkins?'

'Oh yes. The bullets confirmed it. Forensic evidence. Kamrowski and the other two were just low-level bag-snatchers. They had no idea that Carlton was prepared to murder. Perkins must have seen or said or realized something they couldn't tolerate. The police in the States have tracked down Carlton's movements over a period and it all fits. They couldn't answer for his time over here, of course. He was a frequent visitor and it's hard to establish his exact itinerary in England each time.'

She shifted her sitting position in the car, so that I noticed her furrowed brow.

'What I can't work out is: why try to kill Jeremy? That seemed so vicious and so pointless. You, I can understand; you were in the way all the time.' She smiled at me. 'I mean, you were number one to remove.'

'Thank you. Very much. But Jeremy became the motivating force. I work for Jeremy. Jeremy was mad keen to find that painting. With Jeremy removed the major impetus would have gone. And remember: Jeremy was and is in many ways much easier to remove than me.'

'Why?'

'Because I'm a much faster-moving target and I can look after myself. Especially with a guardian angel to watch over me.'

'Flannel! You won't soften me up that way. You're incorrigible. You don't really believe I can protect you at all. And my God, you – we – were lucky.'

'I know. What would I have done without you? You thought of the Sargent connection first. I mean, this whole adventure belongs to you, doesn't it?'

'You bastard! You absolute swine! Don't transfer the responsibility to me! If it hadn't been for you, barging your way around Chicago and New York, nothing would have happened.'

'Of course it would. And remember: Jeremy made me go to Chicago and you made me go to Whitney in New York. To see the Sargent exhibition. Carlton must have nearly had heart failure when I told him I was going there on my afternoon off. Especially to buy the catalogue. No, I think that you and Jeremy must take credit for the whole sequence of events.'

'Tim Simpson, I shall get out of this car *now* if you don't abandon that line of argument!'

That's typical of a woman, of course. They strut about in the background, chi-iking you like mad to do this and do that, handing you the ammunition, pointing out the enemy, sending you over the top at O-six-hundred hours with bayonet in hand, and then when you stagger back bleeding and bloody they say, What, me? Responsible? What on earth can you mean? Have you gone raving mad? I was against the whole thing from the start. I abandoned the conversation; there's no dealing with a woman once she's decided that you are to blame.

'The Cotswolds fooled me for a while. Harry

Howarth kept taking Carlton down to Broadway for the weekend, charging off from Paddington. Right round the corner from Mr Goodston's. Sargent was so often in the Cotswolds and had such connections there that I couldn't help but be suspicious. I thought that the painting might be tucked away in Fladbury Rectory or somewhere like that.'

'How is Howarth? How's he taken it?'

'He's shattered. Absolutely shattered. Carlton was his choice. He kept asking me yesterday, on the phone, if I thought it was the expansion plans that sent Carlton off the rails. Too much for him to handle; that sort of thing. There might have been an element of that, you see. Charles Massenaux warned me after the last meeting that some of the New York managers didn't think Carlton could take a lot of pressure. I don't think it was that. I think he was just mad keen to get the painting for himself and then, when he knew it didn't exist any more, to re-create it.'

'I simply can't believe that he would have got away with a forgery.'

'Not in the long term, no. But as a director of Christerby's, New York, he'd have got his hands on a lot of cash. Look how you all wanted to believe in that painting. Did believe in it. Passionately. Read any history of forgery. It was a natural.'

'Well, we were right, weren't we? It did exist. Had existed. It must have been a terrible blow to Carlton when you confirmed that it had been destroyed at Innishannon.'

'I'm sure it was. He was too far committed, by then, to let us get away. Even if he hadn't wanted to produce a forgery.'

She shivered. 'Don't, Tim. Don't bring up that awful day again. How you anticipated old Coughlan's reaction I'll never know. Come on, let's lay your ghost and call an end to the affair.'

You come into the village of Northiam from the north, after you have crossed the River Rother which divides Kent from Sussex. After a quaint old hump-backed bridge which crosses all that is left of what was once, hundreds of years ago, a wide sea estuary, you follow the road along the flat until it rises up the gentle opposite ridge past the former tiny railway station, to which Edward, Moreton's brother, returned in triumph from the Boer War. The initial approach to the village is flanked by post-war bunga-lows and council estates which belie its rural nature. Like many Sussex settlements, the houses straggle along a ridge for two or more miles, so that you don't reach the church and village green in this case until you are almost at the end, the south side, where Brickwall House sits in the fork in the road. Beyond the house, the park full of oaks stretches into the distance until it meets a double line of chestnuts planted by Moreton's father, Thomas Frewen, to mark the old road to Beckley. In the great brick wall on the Hastings road you can see his initials, T.F. 1838, but Brickwall has had its name since the seventeenth century, when the Frewens first moved into it.

I pulled the car up in front of the high ornamental iron gates and railings at the entrance to the drive that leads to the front of the house. A large three-gabled façade of black-and-white timbering, very uniform in its striping, very handsome in its fen-estration, stood before us.

'That's a very fine house,' Sue said, peering over me. 'What is it now?'

'It's a school. The Frewens made it over to a Trust

after the First World War. Black-and-white timbering is appropriate to Moreton; the Moreton Old Hall he never inherited in Cheshire is much more complex and bendy than this, though.'

'Is it all timbered inside?'

'Oh no, not *all*. There are Renaissance plastered ceilings. The Frewens did a lot to the original house when they moved in. They planted a topiary garden and put up brick walls. Hence the name.'

'Who owned it before them?'

'Oddly enough, a family called White. No relation of Jeremy's. A Frewen forebear became Archbishop of York but the money to buy Brickwall came from a brother in trade, in the City of London. Another Stephen. He bought it from the Whites.'

'This is where Moreton was born?'

'It is. And he's buried in the church back up the road, in a vault under the family chapel. The brothers had private tutors; they didn't go to Eton. With riding wild here and at Innishannon and in Leicestershire, with the avoidance of school food and grinding discipline, it's no wonder they were all a bit over-independent, and tall, and tough. Mr Goodston was right; we shall never turn out anything like the Frewens any more.'

'You and Mr Goodston seem to have formed quite a relationship.' She put her hand on mine and smiled. 'I've never thought of you as a bibliophile.'

'It's a sign of age.'

'Well, there aren't any other signs.' She gave me a meaningful look. 'I can't see you settling down to be an antiquarian book-dealer. Not yet, anyway.'

'Give it time.'

I looked at the house, with its imposing gateposts

capped by lions, its outlying stables, its walled gardens. This was Moreton's start in life, even though he knew it would never be his. What kind of psychological adjustment did a younger son need in those days? 'Some day, my son, all this will never be yours.' You grew up in it and got used to it and just when you had grown up and taken on all its style and bearing and social position they threw you out, into the Army, or the Church, or a dim profession, or something socially suitable. You knew it, of course, you were nothing if not hard-headedly realistic; you knew that the young dog fox must leave the litter and seek its own territory, like those on Ranksborough Gorse that Anita Leslie compared you with, but it must have needed toughness even though, in those days, the whole world was available as a territory. So you rode the prairie, steamed the Atlantic, smoked in the Pullman car, mixed with the string-pullers, frantic with energy to create your own Brickwall, your own place of respect.

'You're talking to yourself. He's really got under your skin, hasn't he?'

'Moreton? I suppose he has, a bit. His nephew, Shane Leslie, was correct. He's a study in sublime failure all right.' I let in the drive and the car moved off. 'Let's go and look at Brede Place, if we can.'

As it turned out, we couldn't. Brede Place is a private house, not the Frewens' any more, but it is still there, an ancient moated place, built of Caen stone brought over by the descendant of some Norman conqueror. It was Clara Jerome Frewen, Moreton's wife, who fell for the dilapidated, uninhabited place in the 1890s and turned it back into a house, even if a wildly impractical house, with no heating, earth closets, freezing cold and draughty and uncomfortable, but wildly romantic and ghost-ridden. She persuaded Edward, who had inherited it with Brickwall, to sell off this one house and some land to her, so that she could make a home she could call her own after all the moonlight flits, the duns, the near-bankruptcy and the bailiffs who were always part of her life. To this, her place, came writers like Stephen Crane, Kipling, Wells and Henry James, politicians with Winston, and, from time to time at first and then more frequently, Moreton, who at last came back to Sussex to die. It had all come to nothing. His money and that of his brothers, his children and his friends and his enemies, had all been spent and lost, vast fortunes of it, gone forever. He used to sit under the huge oak trees and shout that he was dying; it made him angry to think of it, it wasn't fair, nothing that he wanted had come to him after all that effort and absence and risk, all that shrewd intelligence and amazing gift of prediction that he had wasted.

'And yet,' I said out loud, making Sue jump, for she had half joined in my reverie and was staring at the gates to Brede, lost in thought, 'and yet, most people live their lives in boredom and make no money anyway. Poor old Moreton, he did at least live like the splendid pauper that he was. Come on, we'll look at the church and then I will have laid the ghost. Once I've seen the place, somehow my mind settles.'

I turned and drove back to Northiam, parking in front of the old stone church that is entered via a bell-porch. It's quite a big church when you're inside, with a fine oak Renaissance altar rail and so on, but the Frewen family chapel is off to your left, built over a vault where generations of Frewens lie among their forebears.

Sue gave me a roll of her eyes, white in the gloomy

interior. I gestured to the chapel door and we trod carefully across to enter the rather bare, simple annexe through a door in a glass screen. Up on the right-hand side there was a high Victorian marble memorial with mottled brown clustered columns flanking a long inscription. It went up to a Gothic point at the top, with frilly white marble decorations. It was an impressive affair, the biggest in the chapel, as befitted what was probably the most powerful landowner of all the Frewens, the summit of their condition.

'Moreton's father,' I said to Sue, my voice sounding loud in the empty stone chamber. 'You see? That's the old boy who had all the estates.'

We peered upwards at the inscription. *Sacred to the memory of Thomas Frewen, Esq* – that was him all right – *of Cold Overton Hall, Leicestershire; Innishannon, County Cork; and Brickwall House in this parish. Eldest son of John and Eleanor Frewen Turner. Born at Cold Overton Hall, August 26, 1811* – was that why Cold Overton was listed first? Why did it strike a dim chord? – *educated at St John's College, Cambridge* – a Johnian. Must have been a good man – *A magistrate for Rutland and Leicestershire* – hunting country all right, no wonder Moreton was such a horseman – *MP for South Leicestershire in 1832, High Sheriff for Sussex in 1839* – ah, we'd got back to Sussex again.

'*He married first in 1832* – ' Sue's voice suddenly cut in on my thoughts – '*Anne, daughter of W. W. Carus Wilson, Esq. of Castreton Hall, Westmorland.*'

'She died in childbirth while he was taking the waters at Tunbridge Wells.'

'*Secondly* – ' she ignored me – '*in 1847, Helen*

Louisa, daughter of Frederick Homan, Esq. of Hed-
enwood, County Kildare.'

He died at Woodlands, Ore, near Hastings, Oct.
14, 1870.

The solemn text continued, quoting Biblical
extracts. Something was making me frown. I turned
away from the big memorial, which reminded me of
Albert's in Hyde Park, and saw other, simpler tablets,
to other Frewens, ladies, wives, one of Charles Hay
Frewen's wife, Frances.

'She was Moreton's aunt. He – Charles – was the
Uncle Moreton calls pompous and futile in his book.
He lived at Cold Overton Hall until – '

I stopped and walked back to look up at old Thomas
Frewen's big impressive plaque, and there it was, as
it was elsewhere, looking at me. *Sacred to the
memory of Thomas Frewen of –*

Cold Overton Hall.

'What's the matter? You've gone as white as a
sheet. Tim?'

Cold Overton Hall. I sat down on a nearby chair.
Surely that couldn't be right? It must just be a
coincidence.

'Tim? You look absolutely ghastly! For God's sake!
What is it?'

Cold Overton Hall. There had been no coinci-
dences in this whole business. I could see the auction
catalogue in my mind, one that I had sorted in the
office recently. It had a dark green cover with a
photograph of an oak chair on it. The Cold Overton
Hall Collection. Icy chills came up from the stone-
flagged chapel floor. Above me the great frilly-Gothic
memorial pointed its arch at the dark ceiling. Dead
Frewens lay in the mausoleum below my feet. Frewens whom Moreton had rather light-heartedly written

of. Frewens who had taken over the ancient family of Laton. Frewens who had loaned the Adderleys money and taken Innishannon in exchange. Frewens who included Moreton himself, since 1924 permanently down among the vaults. The Cold Overton Hall Collection. America and Ireland and, of course, England. The three places in which most of Moreton Frewen's life had been lived out. His daughter said that he was at heart an American, and should have become one. The Irish would laugh at that and say that he was one of them. But Frewen was an Englishman, whatever that may mean, like me. I hadn't looked nearly hard enough for solutions in England.

'You're shivering! You're not well! Come outside, Tim, quickly! You've gone so white! What is it?'

Cold Overton Hall.

'Get me out. Get me out of here.'

She got her arm under my elbow and I swear she practically propelled me physically through the church, past the bell-porch and out into the greying day.

'You drive,' I said abruptly. 'You drive, Sue. I'm not up to driving. Back to London. Please.'

'What's happened?' She started the car and I switched the merciful heater on full blast. The engine was still warm, thank heaven, and the rush of air struck my face as she moved off, so that my shivering came spasmodically now, instead of full-time as it had been doing. 'Tim! Tell me! What's wrong? You haven't laid a ghost; you look as though you've seen one!'

'Something I hadn't thought of. One of those irrelevant stupidities. An autumn catalogue that I saw. I'll have to get hold of Jeremy; I'm afraid there's much worse to come.'

Chapter Eighteen

The horse whickered in recognition as I scrunched out of the car. It leant its bony brown head over a wooden top rail and stared at me before heaving its nose up and down in what is called a toss. You too, I thought, you give a toss as well, do you, brute?

Jeremy's saloon was already there and he opened the door to save Donald the trouble. 'Tim! Nip in smartly – it's turning chilly at last. Donald's put some coffee on; we're in the kitchen.'

I followed him into the hall and tramped through the dining-room towards the galley-kitchen, where Donald was immured behind his counters to keep out the broth-spoilers. He looked up at me as I walked in. 'Aha! There he is! Come in, young sir, come in. The legend is back. With another scalp to its belt, I hear.'

'Well – hello, Donald. How are you?'

'Not too bad, not too bad. Shocking business. Dreadful. That chap Carlton – who'd have guessed? A director. Member of the Christerby's board. Shocking.'

'Yes, it's been bad.'

'You're all right yourself?'

'Oh yes.'

'And that young lady of yours – Sue whatsername – is she OK?'

'Sue's all right. Fortunately she's tough.'

'Good. Good girl, that. Look here – let's be civilized. Take our coffee to the sitting-room. Better than perching round the counter like a bunch of matelots. Use the vicar's parlour.'

'OK, fine.'

Jeremy picked up a tray loaded with coffee things and sauntered out to a sitting-room beyond an arch, a wide arch that separated it from what I now saw was a dining area rather than a separate room, timbered and half-panelled like the rest of the old house. Donald and Jeremy sat on easy chairs by a low circular table, where Jeremy had parked the tray.

'You take milk?'

'Yes. Thank you.'

Donald sat down in his slightly awkward way, the artificial leg sticking out. He half-turned stiffly to peer at me, twisting his face. 'Well, don't hang back, young feller. Come on. Come and join us.'

'I was just admiring your dresser.' I stared at it where it stood against the wall near the arch, its shelves loaded with willow-pattern plates and its arcaded pot-board decorated with a large tureen in a similar blue-and-white design.

'Oh, that? Fits well, doesn't it?'

'Excellently.' I walked across and joined them, to his evident relief – he settled back more comfortably in his chair – and Jeremy's slight impatience, evident by the way he peered at me with wrinkled brow. 'It's a pity you bought it from our competitors.'

'What?'

'From Sotheby's. It came from Sotheby's, didn't it?'

'What? Yes. Oh yes, I told you, didn't I? The last time you were here.'

'You did indeed. I wondered where I'd seen it before.'

'Really?'

'Yes. I didn't view the sale but I got the catalogue.'

'Have some coffee?' He passed a cup.

'Thanks.' I took it. 'The Cold Overton Hall Collection.'

'Sorry?'

'The Cold Overton Hall Collection. Sold at Sotheby's, Bond Street, on 10th October – this was part of it, wasn't it? I remembered it from the photo in the catalogue. An oak sale.'

'Yes, it was.'

Jeremy put down his coffee to look at me curiously. 'Cold Overton Hall? Wasn't that – '

'The Frewens'? Yes, Jeremy, it was.' I sipped some of mine. 'A long time ago. Cold Overton Hall, Leicestershire. Where Moreton did a lot of his hunting in his early years.'

'Oh yes?' Donald's voice was neutral.

'Yes.' I looked at him as best I could. 'I remembered that Jeremy said your family came from the East Midlands before the war. You rode to hounds there yourself. Until – until you joined up.'

'Yes.' He gave me a stare which implied that I was transgressing, moving on to forbidden ground, the delicate subject of his lost leg.

'You must have known Cold Overton.'

'Not really. We were the other side of Melton. Heard of it, of course. Renowned.'

'It hasn't been the Frewens' for years. Edward had to sell it in 1895 to pay off the debts and mortgages which had accumulated even by then. The agricultural depression and all that.'

'So I believe.'

'Odd that you didn't mention it.'

'I beg your pardon?'

'Considering all the information we were discussing. About Moreton.'

Donald stared at me without blinking. I sensed a shadow crossing Jeremy's face.

'I mean, there we were, rattling on about Moreton and the Frewens while all the time you'd just bought a dresser from Cold Overton Hall. Jeremy admired it specifically, and you never mentioned it. I realize that the place – Cold Overton – had belonged to someone else for years, in fact I remembered it used to be an antique place, I think it was Bill Stokes's. I phoned up Graham Child of Sotheby's – we do talk to our competitors, you know, quite a lot – and he said yes, most of the stuff in that sale had been collected together recently, of course, but the dresser went back a long way. It had always stood in a kitchen servery or something. Went with the house. This was the first time it had been sold separately.'

Donald put down his cup. 'I'm afraid I'm not following the drift of this. What are you getting at?'

'Just that it was odd. You not mentioning it. And I'm afraid I'm bad that way. When I thought about it – I was in Northiam Church, you see, looking at the memorials, and Cold Overton kept coming up, it was an important Frewen possession once – as I say, when I thought about it, I realized that if I hadn't seen that catalogue from Sotheby's, it would never have occurred to me.'

Jeremy's face creased. 'For heaven's sake, Tim. Come to the point, will you? Whatever the point is.'

'Just that if Donald didn't tell us about that, what else didn't he tell us about?'

Jeremy looked from me to Donald with a bewildered expression. Donald had set his features into a hard look, like a yachtsman who was heading into an irritating squall.

'Good heavens, you are a strange fellow. I bought a piece of oak furniture I liked at auction, that's all. The Frewens haven't been at Cold Overton for years. Not for years. They sold it in 1895, as you say. It never occurred to me that there was any significant connection.'

'I'm afraid I think there was. I think that Moreton Frewen and anything to do with him is a very important subject to you.'

Silence. Donald was beady-eyed now, his coffee forgotten. 'I've told you all I know about him. And my father's disastrous investments in his schemes. There's nothing else. I rather resent this.'

'Ah yes, your father. Was it he who told you about the Sargent painting of the Jeromes?'

'What?'

'He saw it, presumably, when Sargent painted his portrait together with his first wife. Around 1900 or so? I got Sue to check, you see. We were thrown the first time, because Sargent painted a White, Mrs George White, she was the American ambassador's wife in London, in 1883, and they were a well-known couple in society. It didn't occur to us at first to look for other Whites. Sue found the reference somehow two days ago. Took her a hell of a time. Your father and stepmother were painted by Sargent. A long time ago. You never told us. But I guess – just guess – that your father must have seen the secret painting of the Jerome sisters and told you. That's why you knew, didn't you, the day I came here and blabbed about the gold shares being kept with a sergeant. You knew it was a Sargent, didn't you?'

'Rubbish! Of course I didn't. What are you implying? Eh?'

'That's why you tried to kill Jeremy. I've thought about that for two weeks. Why would anyone want to kill him? I thought it was because he was pushing me; the motivating force to find that painting. Then I remembered. The day we came here together to ask you about the Sargent, Jeremy was trying to recall something. Something he'd dimly remembered from family talk about a Sargent. It was your father's. That yacht bomb was a military job. The sort you might have learnt in the Army. You didn't want him to remember anything at all.'

'You're mad. Raving mad.'

'You remembered it, though. Very well indeed. If you could get your hands on the three Jeromes, you'd be back in funds.'

'You're mad! It was Carlton who did all that. You proved it yourself.'

'Oh, Carlton was one prime mover, of course. Your partner. I'm afraid Graham Child blew the gaffe on that for you. He was amused when I inquired about the Cold Overton dresser. "What's up with you lot?" he asked me. "Both Jeremy's cousin Donald *and* your New York chap, that new one, Carlton, all after the dresser. Now you, Tim, asking about it. What's the story?" He saw you, you see. Together, you and Carlton, at the sale, buying the dresser. Carlton knew about the Sargent from his research. He was a Sargent freak. You knew about it from your father, and you had all the Frewen knowledge. You pooled your resources. I imagine that he first contacted you when he was doing his research into Sargent's work. He found out about the portrait of your parents in the same way as Sue did. When did he ask you about the painting of the Jerome sisters? He must have raised the subject with you. Didn't he? You knew, of course, that one of the ladies was Moreton Frewen's wife because your father had told you all about that. You were very useful to Carlton and he must have been very useful to you. Mobile and able to supply the materials for the bomb you planted on Jeremy's yacht. That had to be you; one more yachtsman down at Chichester would have been quite unremarkable. Everyone knew you. And you knew Jeremy's yacht of old. Military training has its peacetime uses, especially if you've been in the Armoured Division.'

Donald drew back in his chair. 'This is intolerable! Jeremy, I – '

'If it hadn't been for Moreton Frewen, you'd still be a director of White's Bank, wouldn't you?'

His face changed. I can't describe his expression. It was vile. Horrible. It gave everything away. Unfortunately, I had forgotten to keep a close eye on Jeremy. He spoke, just managing to get the words through his dreadful shock.

'Mary. Mary was with me. You meant to murder her. You – '

I was too late as I jumped to stop him. He's big, is Jeremy, and years of City business lunches have been tempered by strenuous yachting, so that he's not weak, not by any means, and he had Donald by the throat. The flesh bulged over Jeremy's vice-like fingers. It was a horrible couple of minutes, Jeremy roaring in murderous rage, his hands clamped round Donald's throat, Donald shaking and twitching, going white and red and black, me fighting and shouting as I tried to get Jeremy loose, to break his hold.

'Jeremy! Stop! It's not worth it! Let go!'

It was damn near death for Donald. I managed to get between Jeremy's hands, so that, fighting and shouting and hating me, he was finally manhandled off, away, into his chair with me pinning him down. It took all the strength I've got, I can tell you.

'Jeremy, listen! Listen! McIntyre. No, look at me! The puce old johnny. You remember? At the garden party? The one fuelled on Singapore Slings, you said. Him. Major-General McIntyre.

He tried to struggle free, but his face was close to mine and I forced him to look at me. 'What about him? Let me go!'

'His son plays rugger. I contacted him. The General isn't a sawbones any more. He used to be, but he's not, now. His speciality is psychiatry. Psychiatry. He's not a sawbones, Jeremy, he's a shrink. *A shrink*. One of the Army's best, apparently. Donald is a patient of his.'

Jeremy's eyes looked into mine for so long that I had to blink. It was as though he was examining the back of my brain. Then his limbs slackened and I let go of him, so that I could stand up, all ruffled and bruised and shaken, in the middle of the room.

Donald lay in the chair where I had torn Jeremy off him. His artificial leg stuck out at an angle, making him look like a broken doll. His clothes were torn and his face, congested and purple, twitched as he stared at me in hatred. He managed to croak at me, though.

'Smart Alec! Bloody smart Alec! Think you're damn clever, I'll bet.'

'You hate both of us, don't you? As much as Moreton Frewen.'

'Yes I do! If it hadn't been for Frewen bamboozling my father we'd still have had our block of shares in the Bank. We had to sell a lot of them to pay off the debts. Otherwise, we'd still have control. Then you – *you* – wouldn't be strutting about the Bank! You'd be out on your ear, in the gutter, where you both belong! Scum!'

'When did the Sargent go for sale? Of your father, I mean?'

'In the 'forties. My stepbrother needed money. Sargents went for nothing, then.'

'So your father did tell you about the Jeromes painting?'

He leered at me. 'You're so clever! Work it out for yourself!'

'Mary.' Jeremy managed to speak directly to Donald at last. 'I can understand, now, why me. But Mary. My wife. Your bomb would have –'

'Mary!' Donald's voice mimicked him. 'Mary! Your precious wife! That traitress! Uncle Richard's secretary. Feeding you with what you needed in your dirty game to take over the Bank. Stabbing Richard in the back. Working for you, to get me out. Your whore. Your treacherous whore!'

Jeremy leapt, but I had him half way that time. I got him round the waist with both my arms locked and dragged him back, fighting and heaving, to his chair. I had to hold him there for a full two minutes before he stopped, with tears of rage and sorrow on his face. Donald grinned, a horrible grin of triumph and knowledge that made me feel hideously murderous too, but I managed with an effort to straighten up and stare back at him. There was only one weapon I could use against Donald and I had a mind to use it, fairly or unfairly, if he pushed me too far.

He did. 'What can you do?' It was a sarcastic question, put in a triumphant tone.

'Nothing.'

'Nothing? Nothing?'

'No, nothing. This is a family matter. It's not for

me to decide. I am not a member of the family. I shall do nothing.'

He leered. 'What you mean is that you have no proof. No proof you can use. Don't wave the family at me.'

'It's not that.'

My head was in a turmoil. I had planned to hand the whole thing over to Jeremy at that point. He was the boss. It was his family, his feud. I was just a retainer. But Jeremy was sitting stiff in his chair, face congealed. Horror suffused him; his will and nerve were temporarily out of action. I would have to handle this myself. Donald had not only tried to blow Jeremy and Mary to Kingdom Come; he and his accomplice had arranged for that trio to meet me at O'Hare, to kill me if they couldn't get my papers any other way.

'What, then?' Donald's next question goaded me.

'You're not well, Donald.'

'What?' His face changed. A look of unease came over it.

'You haven't been well for years. The Black Dog, you call it, like Winston Churchill. It will do White's Bank no good to have a sensational court case, cousin trying to blow up cousin, spread all over the papers. We can't have that. I prefer the quieter course.'

'What the hell do you mean?'

'We'll talk to General McIntyre. I expect him to explain that the years of pain and frustration have cracked you.'

'You bastard!'

'It'll mean treatment. White's will look after that.'

'Treatment? What treatment?'

'For your own good. A Crown Court would do

precisely the same, so why go to all the trouble and expense and publicity? You can be put quietly away.'

'Wha – I'm not – you –'

'It'll be quite a nice institution. You haven't really got any choice. You're obsessive, Donald. Criminally obsessive. About Moreton Frewen. About the Bank. About Jeremy, and Mary, and me. About your horse and riding. But mostly about Frewen and the financial havoc he wrought on your father's money. The loss of the Bank shares. Buying that dresser was an obsessive act. An act of obsession. It was something of the Frewens from the area where you'd done all your youthful riding. Something the war put paid to. Killing the man who had the gold shares you hoped would provide a clue was obsessive, too; Carlton was like you. I'm sorry for you, actually, Donald.'

'What? You? You dare say that to me?'

'You'll be put in an institution. There won't be any choice once we get to McIntyre. With modern drugs you'll calm down. Eventually. We have to leave, now. This has been a dreadful shock for Jeremy. I'm taking him home. Now.'

I hated this. I had really liked Donald. I hated it. I'd hated it since I'd sat on that chair in the cold Northiam Church, the truth dawning, and Sue had had to drive me home. The shock had affected me. Just as it now had Jeremy. I took him out of the house, telling him he wasn't fit to drive, and I sat him in my car with his pale grey face, speechless. I shut the front door of the house, leaving the interior, with its dresser and Donald stiff inside it, turning over the things I had said to him in my mind. I thought about McIntyre and the Army and Rommel and Donald stuck smashed in his armoured car where it might have been best if he'd died and I shook that thought out of my head. But then the horse whickered in the paddock once again, staring at me, and my thoughts repeated the same line of the verse once more, the verse I'd thought of and Sue had taken up. An unprophetic verse, but it made me shiver as I got into my car to take the silent Jeremy away.

I 'listed at home for a lancer,
Oh, who would not sleep with the brave?
I 'listed at home for a lancer
To ride on a horse to my grave.

Chapter Nineteen

Donald White died the next day in a shooting accident. He took his twelve-bore down the meadow to hunt rabbits, passing the big brown hunter on the way. His daily cleaner saw him stroking the horse's head as he stood talking to it in the middle of the field, letting its big soft lips search him and the pockets of his poacher's jacket for a lump of sugar until he handed one over. She said he was there for quite a while, then she saw him limp away in the grey autumn light. When the shot went off she thought he'd bagged a bunny for the pot. The stable boy found him much later. It seemed that he'd clambered over the fence and his artificial leg had hampered him somehow, caught in a wire on the top rung. He'd fallen and the gun had gone off right into his chest, killing him instantly. It was so unlike Donald, they all said, carrying a loaded and cocked shotgun like that, but he might have seen a rabbit, tried to bag it from the top of the fence and lost his grip or his footing. No one knew. People get careless; it was an accident.

There was a laudatory obituary in *The Times*. The tip of the iceberg, as Mr Goodston would say.

Jeremy didn't speak to me for ten days. He went to the funeral and he came to work erratically, looking pale and tense. I knew he knew that none of it was my fault, I hadn't even started it, but it was a family thing and I had been there, inside it, intrusive. It was hard to take, despite everything we had been through together before. He didn't avoid me obviously, but he didn't speak either, so I stayed away as tactfully as I could until one evening, it was after six and the secretaries had gone, I had to get him to sign some papers. I went into his office, put them in front of him, and while he signed them I stood staring out of the window into the London dark, a London dark full of wet lights, red buses, black taxis and scurrying people heading towards stations to get home. The phone rang and he picked it up, grunting a bit until he turned and spoke to me.

'It's Mary. She says she can't stand this any more and will you and Sue come out to dinner with us tonight?'

'We'd love to.'

He turned back to the phone. 'He says they'd love to. About eight? All right.'

He put the phone down and went across to the cabinet against the wall, pulling a key out of his pocket. 'Drink?'

'Yes, thanks.'

The veneered doors swung open and he peered at the glazed interior, scowling as if in thought.

'Whisky?'

'Yes, thanks. Just ice.'

He nodded absently, picked up a large tumbler, then another one, put ice in both, and then practically filled the glasses with a torrent of whisky. He carried them across to his desk and motioned me to sit down, putting the glasses on the desk-top. As I picked mine up, he reached across with his and touched it gently, causing an icy chink of a toast to sound in the room. I toasted him back silently and drank. He put his glass down after a considerable swallow.

'Making enemies is a vile business.'

'It is.'

'I never believed that Donald – I – I always thought of him as a soldier. And a sort of uncle. A soldier-uncle.'

'I know. If you can, it would be best to leave it like that. Think of him as a soldier, I mean. A long time ago. He was ill, later.'

Jeremy picked up his glass. 'God knows what sort of enemies Moreton Frewen must have made.'

'Mmmm. Obviously, there were some bad ones. Lord Wharncliffe was one. But quite a lot of his losers never seem to have held a grudge, despite lost fortunes. Trades-people must have loathed him. Lowther forgave him; Grey supported him; Donald became obsessive about him.'

Jeremy smiled wryly. 'If he hadn't brought that dresser from Cold Overton, you might never have considered Donald.'

'True.'

'You are an amazing fellow, Tim. Poking about churches.' He cleared his throat awkwardly. 'I've got to ask you something.'

'What?'

'I've had a call from Harry Howarth. The Christerby operation in New York needs a new chief. Someone who can run New York, manage the expansion in Chicago, and probably later in Los Angeles. He asked if he could have you.'

'Me?'

'Yes, you. He says he can't think of anyone better equipped to do it. You understand the art market, you're young, you're tough and you have all the figures in your head. He also says he thinks he can get on very well with you, which is perhaps the most important thing of all. This Carlton business shook him up considerably. He wants someone he can trust.'

Jeremy's face was dark and preoccupied in front of me. I stared at him in some bewilderment. 'What did you tell him?'

'I said that of course I would put it to you. For you to make the decision. It's not that I don't need you here; I do. You know my plans for the Bank. I'm going to need every good man I can get. But I must be fair to you; I don't want you to go, but I must be fair to you. And there's the territorial imperative.'

'The what?'

'The territorial imperative. The male territorial imperative.' He gave me a humorous look. 'You and I are both fairly direct characters, Tim. Sparks are bound to fly. They have flown between us, and they'll fly more as you grow in this business, as you have grown, and take greater things to deal with. Then, to be fair to you, you should have the opportunity of doing your own thing, at least for a couple of years, to prove to the main board that you're not just my dummy, my shotgun guard.'

I opened my mouth, but he held up his hand. 'Don't say anything now. Think about it. A couple of years over in the States, making a go of Christerby's there, would do your career a power of good. You could come back here perhaps and join me in the final putsch to take over White's Bank. It might fit in very well. I can't keep you here, under my wing, for ever. Not for your own good, anyway. And not for both our goods, come to that.'

My first thoughts went to Sue. There was no way Sue would abandon her career at the Tate, not for me. Sue left me once, to go to Australia because of an opportunity there, for a whole year. For her career.

If I went to the States the chances were I'd go alone. It was the classic modern yuppie problem, career versus love, the only difference being that because Sue and I aren't actually married, the legal damage would be minimal. Perhaps it was because of considerations like this, intimations or intuitions she'd had, that she'd always held off marrying me, to limit that sort of damage.

The emotional damage was another matter.

'I thought you and I got on pretty well, Jeremy.'

'We do.' He took it seriously. 'Better, to be honest, than any of my other, er, colleagues. I realize I'm not always easy. But I have to put this to you, Tim. You don't have to take it. There will be other opportunities. It's just that I should draw your attention to Howarth's enthusiasm for you and the opportunity is a good one. I suppose we've never discussed your career strategy until now.'

The young dog fox must leave Ranksborough Gorse. To make the dangerous run to wherever he could find his own territory. Like Moreton Frewen. The world never changes, the laws of nature are supposed to be ineluctable, if that is the right word.

Jeremy was staring at his desk, face dark and gloomy. To hell with nature; it was time to put him out of his misery.

'I've got a low boredom threshold, Jeremy. You said so yourself. I don't see myself as a full-time auctioneer. If it's all right with you, I'll stick around here at the Bank for a bit longer.'

His head jerked up.

'After all,' I went on, 'I'm still on Howarth's board and there are all my other activities to think of, and Sue, and, most important, who on earth will keep you from going barmy? You'd be bored to tears without me here.'

'You're sure?' His face was lightening.

'Positive.'

'My dear Tim! I do realize that you do have other, er, considerations. I – I can't say I'm sorry, but I didn't want to influence you. Poor Howarth is caught very short, though, and you do seem to get on well. Perhaps you could help him temporarily? As I said from the very beginning, we have to get on with this business: expansion into Chicago is vital for Christerby's if they are to get ahead of the competition. There's no time to lose. I – '

His eye caught mine, saw the look in it, and he stopped. A sheepish smile came to his face. There was a pause and then we both burst out laughing, slightly hysterically perhaps, but laughing the laughter of those who need it as much for an emotional release as for the enjoyment of a rich, mutual joke.

Eventually, he managed to stop. 'Here! Have another drink. If we're going to make a night of it, let's make a night of it.'

'Why not?'

He refilled the glasses and held his up in a toast to me. 'Here's to more happy days! That reminds me: something you've never explained.'

'What's that?'

'The painting by Sargent. Of the Jeromes. You've never said who commissioned it.'

'We'll probably never know.'

'But you must have an idea? Come on, Tim, you of all people! Who do you think the gentleman was? Their father, or an admirer? It must have been an admirer, surely?'

'Well, Leonard Jerome died in Brighton in March

1891. I don't think it was him. For once, Brighton had no part in all this, by the way.'

He waved an impatient hand. 'So who was it? Which admirer?'

'Come on, Jeremy. It's not very gallant of you to speculate on such matters. Even old Moreton Frewen could be discreet when it came to affairs of the heart. Perhaps that's why he looked after the painting. Or maybe it was Clara who put it away, not to upset him. Her admirer, King Milan of Serbia, left England in 1897 to go back to his own country, but he continued to write to them both and he didn't die until 1901. He might have sent the commission to Sargent from Serbia and then – he died suddenly – not been able to receive the painting. I do believe it was painted around 1900. Somehow I rule out King Milan, though. That leaves the Duke of Connaught, who had a long and touching affection for Leonie Leslie, and his brother, Bertie himself, Edward the Seventh, who was Jennie's admirer and friend. Jennie would have been married to George Cornwallis-West by 1900. He went off with Mrs Pat Campbell, and she had other admirers, of course. Kinsky was still about – oh hell, there's endless speculation one can go in for. Anyway, this business has taught me a valuable lesson.'

'You? A lesson? What's that?'

I grinned at him and stood up, to be able to stare out at the shiny, wet, dark London outside. 'Digging into the past seems to be a very dangerous business, Jeremy. Besides, you wouldn't want to upset the Royal Family, would you?'